CIRAK'S DAUGHTER

By Charlotte MacLeod

KING DEVIL

WE DARE NOT GO A-HUNTING

CIRAK'S DAUGHTER

CIRAK'S DAUGHTER

❦ ❦ ❦

CHARLOTTE
MacLEOD

Charlotte MacLeod

Atheneum   1982   New York

❦ *For Louise* ❦

Library of Congress Cataloging in Publication Data

MacLeod, Charlotte.
Cirak's daughter.

SUMMARY: An unexpected legacy from the father who
deserted her as a baby starts Jenny on a dangerous
search for answers to questions concerning her father,
his death, and her own future.
[1. Mystery and detective stories. 2. Inheritance
and succession—Fiction] I. Title.
PZ7.M22494Ci   [Fic]   82–1727
ISBN 0–689–30930–9   AACR2

Published simultaneously in Canada by
McClelland & Stewart, Ltd.
Composition by American–Stratford Graphic Services, Inc.,
Brattleboro, Vermont
Manufactured by Fairfield Graphics,
Fairfield, Pennsylvania
Designed by Felicia Bond
First Edition

CIRAK'S DAUGHTER

CIRAK (Ši'răk), JASON PETER
B. Rakovnik, Czechoslovakia, Feb. 11, 1919.
Only son of Vanos & Anna Cirak. Fled to U.S.
to escape Nazi persecution. Rose to sudden
fame through award-winning documentary, *The
Refugees,* filmed with borrowed equipment and
financed by working at odd jobs. Subsequent
films included *Soldier Boy* (1948), *Backhand*
(1952), *Even So* (1958), *Crooked Mile* (1965).
None achieved success of earliest work.
M. Marion Estes Plummer, member of a promi-
nent eastern family, June 1, 1959. One dau.
Jennifer Maria, b. Oct. 29, 1961. Present resi-
dence unknown.

1

"You'd better start watching your diet. I see trouble with the gall bladder."

The woman in the too-tight, too-frilly red satin dress looked at her new neighbor with something close to fear on her pudgy, pasty face. "I'm due to go in for gall bladder surgery a week from Monday," she gasped.

Jenny Cirak gave the woman an I-told-you-so nod and reached for the hand somebody else was eagerly stretching out to her. Gall bladder problems would always be a safe prediction for overweight, middle-aged blondes who'd spent the evening stuffing themselves with chocolates and salted nuts. Jenny'd learned a lot more than she cared to know about women's ailments from her always-complaining female relatives and their hypochondriac friends.

She should have known better than to start this palm-reading act. She'd never done it before, except to amuse the kids at school and once for a church bazaar. She wouldn't have thought of it now if she hadn't been faced with a roomful of strangers all older than she, all wanting to ask personal questions because a newcomer to Meldrum was a big event.

Actually, Jenny hadn't reckoned on being the star attraction when she'd accepted Sue Giles's invitation to a neighborhood get-together. Even saying yes to Sue had taken some courage. It had seemed perfectly obvious then that she'd never have been asked if the Gileses had realized she wasn't Miss Jennifer Plummer, sophisticate, but Jenny Cirak, nineteen and scared stiff.

It was because she believed that, that she was trying to look thirtyish, which wasn't easy for someone who stood exactly five feet tall and weighed a hundred and two pounds if she ate enough jelly doughnuts. She was nervous about her disguise tonight. The sallow makeup and the elaborately curled black wig worked, but the slinky purple cocktail dress didn't. It wasn't glamorous and sexy as she'd thought when she bought it, just a typical teenager's mistake. She might manage better if she didn't try so hard.

In fact, the whole masquerade wasn't turning out as she'd hoped. Back home, battling for her right to come, she'd thought she was embarking on a great adventure. So far, it had been one long anxiety attack.

The fight with her relatives had been mostly force of habit. Ever since Jenny could remember, whenever she'd tried to make a plan for herself, she'd had to defend it tooth and nail—with Aunt Martha scolding, Uncle Fred bellowing, her mother wringing her hands and wailing that she couldn't cope, as if anybody needed to be told. Usually Jenny had been forced to back down, but this time she'd known in advance that she couldn't lose. Jenny didn't have to take anything from anybody, now that she'd inherited Jason Cirak's fortune.

How odd it had felt to be suddenly an heiress; she, Jenny Plummer Cirak, who'd practically crawled on her knees to Uncle Fred for school lunch money. How odd to own an entire house, although a very small one, when she'd had to share her mother's bedroom at Uncle Fred's. How utterly incredible that her wealth had come from the father who'd dumped his wife and child on his in-laws when Jenny was only two years old and never come back to claim them.

Strangest yet was the fact that Jason Cirak, bohemian, cosmopolite, and famous motion picture director, should have met his end in Meldrum. Whatever had he been doing in this sleepy corner of Rhode Island, tiniest of all the fifty states?

Granted, Cirak was a has-been. The documentary film that had rocketed him to fame years before Jenny was born didn't even get shown on late-late television any more, and few could recall a single title of his subsequent pictures.

The money he'd made, and there had been a lot of it, had been flung high, wide, and handsome across three continents. At least the Plummers had assumed Jason must be throwing his wealth around. He'd never spared any for the wife and child he'd so carelessly acquired and so soon discarded on his frenetic journey through life. He'd known the Plummers were rich and respectable, so Marion and the baby would not starve; and he'd taken advantage of that fact just as he appeared to have taken advantage of everything and everybody he'd ever run across.

After his last box-office disaster, Cirak had slid out of sight. For years the family hadn't known whether he was dead, in jail, or sponging on some new sucker. Consequently, the lawyer's letter had come as a terrible shock.

"Where did the money come from?" Uncle Fred had roared. "That's what I want to know."

That was what all the Plummers wanted to know. Either Jason had been holding out on Marion all those years, while her brother thought he was too broke to sue for nonsupport, or else he'd been up to something.

If so, what? Had he involved the family in a crooked deal by wishing off his ill-gotten gains on Jenny? And why Jenny? Why not Marion, who was still his lawfully wedded and never divorced wife? Why not Fred with Martha, who'd raised his brat for him?

Jenny had endured the ranting and raving for five days before it dawned on her that she didn't have to stand it any more. Then she'd gone, all on her own without telling anybody, to the lawyer's office. When she came back, she had a brand-new checkbook in her purse and a compact car on order. That was the boldest thing she'd ever done in her life. Naturally, Uncle Fred had hit the ceiling when he found out.

"Are you out of your mind? You don't know anything about handling money."

Jenny had stuck to her guns. "I know a little more now than I would have if I'd depended on you to teach me. I'm going to Meldrum as soon as I can get my car on the road. I'll stay in my house there until I find out what my father was doing and where he got the money he left me."

"Ridiculous! You can't go tearing off by yourself like that."

"Why not? I passed my driver education and got my license two years ago. I have plenty of cash. Mr. Delorio the lawyer says I'm old enough to do as I please. And if you give me a hard time, I'm to let him know, so you'd better not try to stop me."

Uncle Fred wasn't about to buck a lawyer. He had to content himself with snarling, "That's the thanks I get," and stalking off to sulk in his den.

Her mother had dealt with the situation in her usual way, by bursting into tears. "At least let Aunt Martha go with you," she'd pleaded. "I'd go myself, but I'm simply not up to it." Marion never was.

"No, Mother," Jenny had insisted. "Aunt Martha doesn't want to go, and I don't want her. If I go trooping down there with all my relatives, I'll never find out anything. I'm better off alone."

Surprisingly, Aunt Martha herself had agreed. "Oh, let her go and make a fool of herself if she wants to. We can't stop her anyway, and I certainly don't want her lolling around here playing the fine lady and expecting to be waited on hand and foot."

That was a dig at Marion, who cried all the harder and said so.

"Oh, turn off the waterworks, Marion. Jenny can write

and let us know how she's making out. No sense in running up long-distance phone bills, even if she has money
to throw around on a wild goose chase."

Jenny had dropped her mother a note last night, saying that she'd gotten here safely, that the house was reason-
ably comfortable, that Meldrum seemed like a pretty quiet
little place, and that there was a Congregational Church
on the next corner. These facts ought to satisfy the Plummers that she wasn't trapped in some den of vice, not that
they were really much concerned.

She knew why Aunt Martha had backed her up about
coming here alone. Aunt Martha had always resented
Jenny's presence in the house and would have grabbed
almost any excuse to get rid of her. On the other hand,
Aunt Martha had also wanted to keep on Jenny's good
side in case the inheritance turned out to be legitimate.
She and Uncle Fred respected money, even if it had come
from Jason Cirak, and even if they'd had a hard time
getting Mr. Delorio and the other lawyers to admit it had.

The Plummers didn't seem to be greatly interested in
the circumstances that puzzled Jenny most: that Jason
Cirak had been living in Meldrum under the name James
Cox, and that he'd made his bequest to his daughter
through a devious rigmarole of trust funds so that the
identities of the donor and the legatee wouldn't have to
be revealed to the general public. Uncle Fred had simply
concluded, with a twinge of envy he hadn't quite managed to hide, that Jason had found a smart way to dodge
taxes.

Whatever the reason for her father's cloak-and-dagger
life and will, Jenny was grateful now for the screen it

gave her. She'd never known any James Cox, and she could say so in all sincerity. Anyway, why should she suspect his motive when she was doing her utmost to conceal her own identity for a perfectly innocent reason?

She wished she could have chosen a different name, but she'd had to remain Jennifer Plummer because it was on the driver's license she'd no doubt have to show sometime for identification. Should anybody question the Cirak part, she was going to say she'd been divorced and gone back to using her maiden name, though she hoped she'd never have to tell such a barefaced lie.

As to what she was doing in Meldrum, Jenny had decided to pretend she was an author in search of a quiet place to write. That was only half a lie. Jenny did like to write, and the role should be easy to sustain. Everybody knew authors were odd creatures who lived in strange places and never really did any work, but slopped around in bathrobes drinking quarts of coffee. If anybody came to the door, she could start pecking frantically at her typewriter and pretend she'd been at it for hours. That was no problem. It was the detective work that mightn't be such a breeze.

Jenny was finding the going sticky right now. The new hand that had been thrust under her nose was hairy on the back, moist on the palm, overly padded on the mounts, and making playful grabs at her fingers.

"I'm glad I'm not married to you," she blurted out because she was too annoyed to be tactful. "Your wife must have a heck of a time keeping her eye on you."

Somebody guffawed. "Look out, Greg! She's got your

number. Hey, Jenny, you're not getting to read my palm. I wouldn't risk it."

"Are you a professional palmist?" somebody else was asking.

"Oh, no," Jenny mumbled. "I just do it for fun."

Of which she wasn't having much right now. Little did they know that she seldom even remembered which line was supposed to represent the heart and which the head. She went by her general impressions, the subjects' reactions to what she told them, and that overdeveloped intuition the Plummers always referred to with nervous loathing as the Cirak streak in her.

So Grabby-Fingers here was Greg. She ought to be making an effort to remember names and faces. She'd be running into these people at the supermarket and whatnot, no doubt. Snubbing one of them would be a marvelous way to turn the entire pack against her and keep them from telling her what she'd come to find out.

They'd know her, no fear of that. Catching sight of her reflection in the Gileses' gilt-edged mirror, Jenny was aghast to see what she'd turned herself into. That mass of fake black hair on her head, combined with the flashy purple dress and the over-lavish makeup, had deepened her ivory complexion to dull gold and her dark brown eyes to coal black. She looked exactly like the sort of woman she'd seen through dingy storefront windows, beckoning from behind signs that read, "Madame Zara. Sees all, tells all." No wonder they were taking her for a professional fortune-teller. What else were they thinking about her?

Jenny felt sick to her stomach, but she didn't dare get up and leave. The damage was already done; might as

well stick it out to the bitter end. She stammered a few
less inflammatory remarks to Greg, then turned to her
next customer.

At least she wasn't likely to put her foot in it here.
This was a lady's hand: fragile, thin-skinned, blue-veined,
freighted with diamond rings in old-fashioned settings. It
could only belong to Mrs. Firbelle, who owned the handsome, pillar-fronted estate to which Jenny's little remodeled carriage house had once belonged.

"I'm sure you don't see much of a future for me, Miss
Plummer." Mrs. Firbelle's laugh was a silvery tinkle, like
her voice. "At my age, a woman has only a past, and I'm
afraid mine hasn't been a particularly exciting one."

Jenny traced the lines in the palm with her own index
finger. That always helped her to get the feel of the personality, though she couldn't have explained why.

"No," she contradicted. "Your life is far from over."
That was a safe enough guess. Mrs. Firbelle couldn't be
much over sixty-five and obviously took excellent care of
herself.

"You're in good health except for a touch of arthritis."
The skin was clear and the bumps at the finger joints
hardly noticeable.

"You react strongly to beauty." That gown she had on
was a work of art, at any rate.

"Your life has been a happy one in many ways," or
should have been, in that lovely home with plenty of
money to run it as she pleased.

"But you have known great sorrow." Any woman was
bound to have suffered some tragedy or other at her age,
unless she'd lived under a glass bell all these years.

"The loss of a loved one." A slight contraction of the

slender fingers told Jenny she was on target. Mrs. Firbelle's husband had been dead for many years, Sue Giles
had told her, so that wouldn't have been the death she
was still mourning. A more recent bereavement, then?

"I think you've had more than one tragedy in your
life. Perhaps not too long ago, something happened that
hit you harder than you've let anyone know." Diamonds
and silver brocade hardly suggested mourning, but the
entire hand was rigid now.

"Mama" interrupted a thinnish brunette in a blue linen
shift, "shall I bring you a glass of sherry?"

"Not just now, Pamela. I'm having my fortune told."
Mrs. Firbelle's tone made subtle fun of the young palmist.
"Well, Miss Plummer, is that all you have to tell me?"

The barb went in, the Cirak streak came out. "No, it
isn't."

Jenny bent closer to the tissue-paper palm. That queer
little red mark on the so-called life line couldn't possibly
have any meaning, of course, but she could not prevent
herself from speaking.

"There's danger around you. I don't think it's an accident. I think there's someone who's plotting to—oh, I
don't know what it means, but the danger is near you. I
can feel it!"

Whatever had possessed her? Jenny dropped the hand
because her own was trembling with fear and shame.
Mrs. Firbelle only laughed.

"The gipsy's warning. How dramatic. Thank you so
much, Miss Plummer. Pamela, I'll have that sherry now,
please."

2

"Why did you try to scare Mrs. Firbelle?"

A tall redhead she'd heard them call Larry was scowling down at Jenny from behind a silly handlebar mustache. She scowled back.

"I wasn't trying to scare her. I tell what I see, that's all."

"Sure you do. Can I get you a drink?"

"No, thanks. I have to go home." All Jenny wanted now was to get out of there before she made a fool of herself again. "There's so much to do, getting settled," she half-apologized, to save face.

"Hey, Jenny, can't it wait till tomorrow? You're not running out on us so early?"

That was Greg, the man with the sweaty palm. He had it wrapped around her elbow now. Jenny wished he didn't. Aside from the fact that she hated being pawed, she had a hunch Greg was Pamela's husband. That would make him Marguerite Firbelle's son-in-law. Letting him make a pass at her in front of the neighbors would really put the frosting on the cake. Jenny panicked and tried to pull away.

Surprisingly, Larry came to her rescue. "I got here first, Greg. She hasn't read my palm yet. How about it, Miss Plummer?"

Greg shrugged, pasted a good-sport grin to his handsome but jowly face, and melted into the crowd.

"I'm not reading any more palms tonight," said Jenny. "Anyway, you don't really want me to."

Larry only shrugged.

"Then I'll ask you to excuse me. I must find Mrs. Giles to say good night."

"Sue's in the kitchen laying out a spread she's spent the past three days getting ready, and she'll hate you forever if you don't stay to eat it."

"But I've been eating ever since I got here," Jenny protested. "I've never seen so much food in my life."

"You must find our native customs too quaint for words. What brought you to Meldrum, anyway?"

"I came here because the people are so charming and friendly," she snapped. Then she turned her back on him and began talking to one of the plump and curious matrons she'd been trying all evening to dodge.

That was a stupid remark to make, Jenny realized as soon as it was too late. If she was going to start picking fights with every man she met, she might as well have stayed at Uncle Fred's.

At least she'd managed this time to pick a companion

who wanted to gossip. "I see you've met our handsome bachelor," the plump woman was saying with a coy giggle.

"Have I? I've met so many people here that I'm afraid I've lost track of who's who. Do you mean that distinguished-looking gray-haired man standing over by the door?" Jenny knew perfectly well she didn't.

"Heavens, no!" The woman was laughing so hard now that it must be putting a terrible strain on her girdle. "That's my husband. I meant Lawrence MacRae, that redhead you were talking with just now."

"Oh, the one with the mustache. I'm sorry, I thought you said handsome." It was a feeble effort, but Jenny couldn't come up with anything better at the moment. "What does Lawrence MacRae do?"

"Good question. He calls himself a roving photographer. I can believe the roving part, all right."

Well, MacRae needn't rove Jenny Cirak's way, not that he showed any sign of wanting to. Now he was trying out his charm on a squealy blonde who hadn't let Miss Plummer read her palm because it was too scary.

"My husband's the town druggist," her new chum was informing her. "He's Sam Green and I'm Daisy. Sue introduced us before, but I expect you don't remember. I was named after Aunt Marguerite," Daisy added with a self-satisfied nod at the woman in silver brocade.

"Mrs. Firbelle?" Jenny was surprised. "Then you're a cousin to that pretty, dark-haired woman they call Pamela."

"Pamela Bauer, yes. She's Aunt Marguerite's daughter. That's Pam's husband Greg over at the bar."

"I thought it was," Jenny said. "I just read his palm."

"Watch out he doesn't try to read yours. Pam's got her hands full with that boy, between you and me. Greg has to watch his step, though. He knows Aunt Marguerite wouldn't stand for any monkey business."

Daisy's remark might be vague, but her meaning was clear. Mrs. Firbelle must control the family money and make them all toe the mark, just as Uncle Fred did with the Plummers. She couldn't be any freer with the funds than he was, either. That was a tacky dress Daisy had on, and Pamela's was no better quality, though more smartly cut.

"And that's my cousin Jack, Pam's brother. Jack's not too well, and he lives at home with his mother. And the woman next to him, in that pink crocheted outfit, is our cousin Beth. She's staying with Aunt Marguerite, too."

Beth must be a poor relation, Jenny thought. The hideous shrimp-pink top and skirt were inexpertly worked and clumsily put together. Beth had made a bad job worse by crocheting a droopy stole and a drawstring bag that hung over her arm on a lumpy cord of the same ugly color. She was thin and inclined to stoop and had the anxious-to-please look of somebody who lived on another's bounty.

Right now, Beth was bringing a daintily arranged plate from the buffet for her aunt. Jack came along to arrange pillows and fetch a tray table so that his mother could eat in all possible comfort. How nice. Everybody was related to Mrs. Firbelle, it appeared, or to someone connected with her. Sue Giles, the hostess, was Daisy's husband's sister. The giggly blonde with Larry MacRae was Sue's cousin's wife. The cousin himself, an airline pilot, was off in the wild blue yonder tonight, according to Daisy. That

must be why the wife was acting so flighty with the
photographer.

MacRae was not related to anybody except his grandmother, who lived two streets over and couldn't come to
the party because her cat was sick. He had arrived late
because he'd taken the cat to the vet, who was a brother-
in-law of Greg Bauer. Jenny never got to find out whom
the grandmother's cat was related to because Daisy
couldn't wait any longer to wade into the buffet.

She herself would much rather have skipped it, but
she didn't dare resist Sue's urgings to "Try some of this.
It's my special recipe." By the time people started to collect their wraps and she could leave without offending her
hostess, Jenny was stuffed to the eyeballs and none too
comfortable in her stomach. The Firbelles' insistence on
walking her home didn't make her feel any better.

There was no real reason why they should. She could
have nipped through the hedge and been there in two
seconds, but Mrs. Firbelle made a stately little procession
of it. Beth had time to let Jenny know the soil around the
carriage house was no good for roses, but that the yarn
shop in the village was excellent. Jack snarled about the
condition of the asphalt sidewalk and the general in-
competence of the Meldrum Board of Selectmen. Mrs.
Firbelle asked what Miss Plummer did when she wasn't
reading palms.

This must be what they'd come fishing for. "I'm trying
to be a writer," Jenny answered with her fingers crossed.

Jack snorted. "Rather a picturesque way of starving to
death, isn't it?"

"Oh, well," said Jenny, trying to sound blasé, "I expect my trust funds will keep the wolf from the door."

"But what if it happens to be a very large wolf?" tinkled Mrs. Firbelle.

"Luckily for me, it was a very large inheritance. I was the only child."

"Oh."

Now they'd heard what they wanted to know. And the Firbelles weren't about to snub an heiress. Beth waxed more eloquent about rose sprays, Jack more waspishly Establishment. Mrs. Firbelle made hospitable noises about a simple dinner with the family. At last, Jenny had said the right thing.

She was beyond feeling pleased with herself. The late hour, the surfeit of food, the strain of having to play her role in front of all those strangers had exhausted her but left her too keyed-up to sleep. After she'd locked up the carriage house and gotten ready for bed, she wandered around the small rooms, picking things up and putting them down.

These were things her father had touched, had handled, had lived with. Jenny had never been able to hate him as much as they'd tried to make her. How could you blame a man for running away from the Plummers? All she'd ever minded was that he hadn't taken her, too. Always, there'd been her private dream that some day he'd come back to get her. Perhaps he'd meant to. Anyway, he'd done the next best thing. Had he pictured her here in the carriage house, the way she was trying to picture him?

She knew what Aunt Martha would say to that. How could he, when he'd never taken the trouble to find out what she looked like? She'd never seen so much as a snapshot of him, either. Uncle Fred had destroyed any her mother might have had.

"Why should you bother your head about him? He doesn't give a hoot about you."

But he had cared. No matter how her father had managed to get hold of all that money—even if she wound up having to kiss her inheritance goodby—she'd have the comfort of knowing he'd wanted her to have it. Where was he buried? How had he died? Oh, why did he have to leave her before she'd gotten a chance to know him?

Jenny was at the kitchen window now, looking out at the pattern of bare branches against the blue-black of a late October sky. The moon was on the wane. High wisps of cloud that meant winds to come threw a milky haze across its lopsided pale-gold oval. She was chilly, standing in her thin nightgown with only a nylon peignoir thrown over it. Did the furnace work, she wondered. Maybe she ought to have it checked.

How strange to own a furnace, she who'd never owned anything bigger than a schoolbag in all her life. How strange to be here by herself, having to make her own decisions instead of being surrounded by a herd of Plummers telling her she couldn't.

She was finished with the Plummers. Jenny had known as soon as she'd backed her new car ever so carefully out of Uncle Fred's driveway that she was never going back, not really. She'd pay token visits on holidays, she supposed, and send her mother a check now and then. If it wound up in Fred's pocket instead of Marion's purse, that was their business. Jenny had no noble intention of pay-

ing him and Aunt Martha back for what they'd be-
grudged her all these years, as if it had been their personal money they were spending instead of funds left in
trust for the entire family. They could keep Jenny's share
of the Plummer money from now on. They weren't getting any of Jason Cirak's, if she could help it.

From the kitchen, she had a view of the Firbelles' back
yard, an acre or more of well-tended garden backing up
to the shaggy little plot she was entitled now to call her
own. The rear of the house, sitting up on the knoll at the
far end, was less imposing than the front, but it still
looked elegant and important, like Mrs. Firbelle. It was
a good thing Jenny'd been able to give the right answer
when the matriarch dropped that ever-so-gentle hint
about the state of her bank account, she thought. If she
didn't have so much money, she'd most likely have got
dropped flat on her face after that stupid palmistry act.
Whatever had possessed her to add that ridiculous bit
about danger?

Though maybe it wasn't so ridiculous. Jenny had always found her hunches pretty reliable, and she'd heard
enough cynical remarks from the Plummers to believe a
wealthy widow with a gaggle of poor relations might
have real cause for worry.

Judging from the little Jenny had seen of her at the
party tonight, Mrs. Firbelle expected plenty of attention
from her relatives. If the contrast between her clothes and
the younger women's, particularly poor Beth's, was any
indication, though, she didn't give much back. Furthermore, she was adept at slipping in the needle where it

hurt, as Jenny had reason to know. No doubt a lot of other people around Meldrum did, too.

Wasn't this fun, standing here in the dark scaring herself silly! If she was going to make up awful stories about rich old ladies in big houses, maybe that book she was pretending to write ought to be a gothic novel. Actually, it might be interesting to try one.

"Gianna stood at the window of the old carriage house, her raven hair in wild disarray, her exquisite features frozen into a mask of terror. Was that a human form she spied lurking in the shadows of the haunted mansion?"

Jenny caught her breath. Had she talked herself into imagining things? Or was somebody actually standing out there under that big maple tree, next to the low picket fence that marked the boundary between her yard and the Firbelles'?

Probably just Beth taking the family dog for its outies, she tried to tell herself. But her neighbors didn't have a dog; at least she hadn't seen or heard one so far. Anyway, Beth had looked pretty frazzled around the edges by the time they'd said good night. She must be in bed by now.

It wasn't tall enough to be Jack, she thought. Besides, since Jack wasn't a well man, he'd hardly be dawdling around outdoors at this hour. Surely it couldn't be Mrs. Firbelle. Even in silhouette, that stately little form should have been unmistakable. And Jenny wasn't even sure whether it was a man or a woman over there.

She felt the short hairs on her head begin to prickle. Why hadn't she thought of getting a watchdog before it was too late? By now, everybody in Meldrum must have heard there was a young single woman living in the carriage house. If that was in fact a prowler planning to break into her house, she could be in real trouble. And if she let him scare her any worse than she was scared already, she might as well fold up and quit right now.

Without giving herself time to think twice, Jenny snatched a heavy, silver-knobbed walking stick out of the umbrella stand and slipped out the back door. As the night wind caught her thin robe, she realized what an utter fool she was being. At least she might have had sense enough to put on a coat over her nightgown.

But if she went back to get one, she'd never find the nerve to come out again. Taking a firmer grip on the cane that must have been her father's, Jenny sneaked forward. The moon was wholly behind the clouds now, and she'd lost sight of the figure. There! No, only a bush. Maybe the person had seen her come out and run away. She moved a bit more boldly.

"Going somewhere, Miss Plummer? Rather late to be out for a stroll, isn't it?"

She recognized the voice and the silly mustache. It would have to be Lawrence MacRae. On his way home from bidding the blonde a cozy good night, no doubt.

"I saw somebody on the lawn," she explained stiffly.

"So you came rushing out with a club to say hello."

"I thought it was a burglar. I have this little hangup about not getting murdered in my bed." She clutched the billowing folds of her flimsy peignoir around her as best she could and moved back toward the carriage house, feeling as foolish as she must be looking. MacRae blocked her way.

"Miss Plummer, I don't know what sort of game you're

trying to play here, but if your plan is to throw a scare into Maggie Firbelle, you might as well forget it. She's a lot tougher than you are. By the way, you've forgotten to put your hair on."

"Oh, sh-shut up!"

"Would you care to tell me what this is all about?"

"I told you, and you didn't believe me. Let me b-by. I'm freezing."

He let her move on, but stuck right with her as far as the door.

"Mind if I come in a minute?"

"Yes, I do mind," she blazed. "I don't know what you think I am, Mr. MacRae, but there's one thing you can be very sure I'm not."

She got a little satisfaction out of slamming the door in his face.

3

Hot milk, aspirin, and the warmth of her bed after the two-way chilling she'd gotten sent Jenny to sleep at last. She didn't wake up until somebody rang her doorbell at half-past ten the next morning. With any luck, it was the plumber about that leak in the basement, though he'd said it'd be a week or ten days, since it wasn't an emergency. She threw on a bathrobe, pulled a comb through her hair, and ran to let him in.

"Oh, I beg your pardon. I'm afraid I've got you out of bed."

Jenny blinked. This couldn't be the plumber, surely, or the Avon lady or the minister's wife. A tall, middle-aged woman in elegant tweeds, clutching a gold-mounted attaché case and a marvelous alligator handbag was standing on the front stoop, looking pleasantly apologetic. She must have the wrong house.

Jenny smiled back. "You did, but it's quite all right. I should have been up ages ago. I just moved in, and I've knocked myself out trying to get settled."

"You've just moved in?" Why should the stranger look so upset by that remark? "But you do come from around here? Recently married, perhaps?"

"No, I'm not married, and I'm from out of state."

"Oh, then you came to be near friends or relatives?"

"No, I don't know a soul except some neighbors I met last night." This was none of the woman's business, of course, but she did look so respectable and so disturbed that it seemed rude to brush her off. "So if you're looking for directions or something, I'm afraid you've picked the wrong house. I'm sorry I can't help you."

Jenny began to inch the door closed, but the woman made no move to leave. "I can't have the wrong house. See, here it is. Eighty-three Packard Road, Meldrum, Rhode Island."

Jenny looked at the wrinkled scrap of brown wrapping paper the woman took out of that magnificent handbag and shook her head. "How odd. I certainly never wrote that, and the house stood empty for six months before I moved in. Could there be another street with the same name around here, I wonder?"

"The men at the fire station said no. I stopped there for directions, and they told me it must be this place. An old carriage house, remodeled, they said. There isn't another one like it, is there?"

Jenny shook her head. "I'm sorry. I wish I could help you. Would you like to use my phone to call a cab or anything?"

She didn't see any car out front and there was no public transportation in Meldrum, so she concluded the woman must either have walked from somewhere or come in a taxi and let it go, assuming she'd found the right address. The Plummers would have fits if they knew she was inviting a total stranger into the house, but somehow this pleasant, middle-aged woman felt more like a friend to her.

"That's tremendously kind of you. I shouldn't impose."

In spite of her polite demurrer, the woman followed Jenny into the house. "What a delightful little place you have here."

"Thank you, but please don't think I picked out the furniture. I'm going to get rid of those red and yellow cauliflowers as soon as I have a chance to shop for draperies and slipcovers. I—took the house already furnished."

"Some people do tend to confuse clutter with coziness." The unexpected visitor dodged a lurid jardiniere full of pampas grass and motheaten peacock feathers. "But I'm sure it will be delightful once you get weeded out here."

She gave an approving nod to the blue-checked cloth and the copper mug full of late marigolds with which Jenny had tried to spruce up the table in the tiny breakfast nook off the kitchen.

"I'm trying to think what to do. I've apparently chased a wild goose all the way from Baltimore."

"Baltimore, Maryland!" Jenny exclaimed.

"How many Baltimores are there? I don't know what I came looking for, but I'm sure it wasn't you."

How could she be sure? Jenny knew the paper meant nothing to her personally, but who was to say it didn't have some connection with the mystery surrounding her father? She made a quick decision.

"I'm going to put on some coffee for us and go get some clothes on. Please sit down. I shan't be a second."

"Do you really want me to? I didn't mean to involve you in this."

"Please."

The woman gave Jenny a quick smile, then sat down and folded her well-kept hands on the blue tablecloth. When Jenny came back in jeans and a red jersey, she was still sitting, as if she hadn't moved a muscle. Jenny rattled cups, and she came out of her abstraction with a start.

"I'm sorry, I should have introduced myself. My name is Harriet Compton." She gave a Baltimore street address that meant nothing to Jenny. "I'm a certified public accountant by profession."

"How do you do?" Jenny replied automatically. "I'm Jenny—Plummer, and I'm trying to be a writer."

"Would I have read any of your work?"

"I don't see how. I've never had anything published, except in my school newspaper. I'm just getting started, that's why I moved here. It seemed like a nice quiet place to write."

"I see." Was there a hint of a twinkle in Miss, or Mrs. Compton's shrewd blue eyes? "You're fortunate to have the knack of putting words together. I don't, obviously, or I'd have thought of a sensible way to explain what I'm doing here."

She took the cup of coffee Jenny poured out for her and helped herself to a doughnut. "Thank you. These look delicious. Well, now that I've worked myself up to it, I don't know whether to tell you or not. You'll no doubt think I'm stark raving."

Anybody saner looking than this elderly business-woman from Baltimore would have been hard to picture. She'd slipped off her beautifully tailored, silk-lined jacket to reveal a hand-embroidered beige blouse and a double strand of what were surely real pearls. The gray hair that showed under her rust-colored felt hat was cut in a crisp swirl that suited her longish, strong-featured face. She was the sort of woman who hadn't gotten asked to the senior prom, but had aged into distinction while the class beauty was settling down as a middle-aged frump.

"I'm not going to think anything of the sort," Jenny replied. "Anyway, you've got to tell me now. Do you mean to say you've come all this way just on account of that piece of paper?"

"That's what I did. I flew up to Providence and squandered a fortune on a taxi to bring me to Meldrum. As to what prompted my trip . . ." She fumbled with the catch of her attaché case, opened the lid, and pulled out a bulky tan something or other. "Here it is. This was in the bundle."

"A suede jacket?" Jenny stared at the article Miss Compton had spread out for her to see. "It must be a man's, from the size and cut. But what's so—it's not very clean, is it? What's that stain on the front?"

"What does it look like?"

"Chocolate ice cream? No," Jenny frowned at the stiffened, dark brown discoloration. "It wouldn't be blood, by any chance?"

"I should have waited till you'd finished your breakfast."

"No, that's all right. I'm not squeamish." Jenny took a quick swallow of coffee to prove it. "But where did it come from?"

"Here, I assume. Somebody mailed it to me."

"Whatever for?"

"That's what I came here hoping to find out. I told you it was going to sound crazy, didn't I? Last Tuesday morning, the mailman rang my bell. I went down, and he handed me a parcel done up in rather scroungy-looking brown paper. I wasn't expecting anything, but it had my name and address on it, so of course I took it."

"There doesn't happen to be any other Compton living in your neighborhood?" Jenny suggested. "They might have looked up the name in the phone book and picked the wrong person."

"I thought of that, naturally, but there isn't. Anyway, there was no return address on the outside. I remember standing there in the hallway wondering if maybe this was a present from one of my former clients. I do get them once in a while, though people don't usually look on their accountants as warm personal friends. We're too closely associated with debits and taxes. But to make a long story short, I took the package back upstairs to my apartment and opened it. The jacket was inside, not even properly folded and packed. So I knew the score even before I saw the bloodstains."

"Then you're smarter than I am," said Jenny. "I still don't see any sense to this."

"That's because you haven't been around as long as I

have. Okay, Miss Plummer, suppose you suddenly found yourself stuck with a piece of clothing you didn't dare have found in your possession. It's too big to hide, too conspicuous to throw away, and too tough to burn. How do you get rid of it in a hurry? Wrap it up and mail it to an out-of-state address."

"But couldn't you just have it dry-cleaned?"

"Maybe you wouldn't dare."

"Oh. Then you—" She thought of the things Uncle Fred had said about her father and took another gulp of coffee. "You think this jacket was worn by somebody who committed a—a crime?"

"Can you think of any other explanation?"

"I can't think at all. Would you like some more coffee, Miss Compton?"

"Yes, please. Let me just get this thing out of sight. It's not very pretty."

The older woman folded the jacket again, so the stains wouldn't show, and laid it behind her on top of the attaché case. "As you may imagine, I've been giving the matter a good deal of thought. I did think of taking the jacket down to the police station, but to tell you the truth, I didn't want to. They'd probably have thought I was just another scatty old dame trying to get some attention. Besides, it was my problem, not theirs."

She laughed a little at herself. "I've pretty much retired lately, you see, and it's a boring, depressing business if you want to know. An old workhorse like me doesn't take kindly to the leisure life. That suede jacket was a blessing, in a way. It's given me something to think about besides my troubles. I worked up all sorts of theories. I fished in the pockets, fiddled around like a kid with a new toy. I don't know why I didn't think right away to unfold the wrapping paper, but I didn't, until day before yesterday. It had been doubled over, you see. And that's when I found your address. I suppose the wrapping was originally used on something that was delivered here. You know how a shipper will often write the address but not the name on a bundle that's being delivered by truck, for the driver's convenience."

"Yes, and then the person who gets the package folds up the wrapping paper and sticks it away in a closet because you never know when it might come in handy." Aunt Martha Plummer had acres of used wrapping paper.

"Exactly. The person who mailed off this jacket may have used this particular sheet simply because it happened to be kicking around ready to hand. If he was in a hurry, he mightn't have thought to unfold it and make sure there was nothing written on the inside. He might even have been working in the dark when he wrapped it up and added the address on the outside later."

"But why yours, Miss Compton?"

"Don't ask me, Miss Plummer. Maybe it was just happenstance, or he might have picked my name out of a Baltimore phone book. You don't have one in the house here, by chance?"

"The place is so cluttered, I don't know what I've got," Jenny replied. "I don't recall having seen one, but I'll hunt around."

"Thanks. If you could find one, it would indicate that the jacket could have been sent from here."

"But I told you nobody's lived here for months."

"I know, but someone could have broken in. And there must be a real estate agent or a lawyer or someone who had access to the place while it was vacant.

"I—yes, certainly. I hadn't thought of that," said Jenny. "Sometimes people leave keys under the doormat or somewhere. For all I know, the whole neighborhood might have been running in and out." The thought wasn't a pleasant one. "I think I'll have the locks changed."

"Haven't you done that already?" Miss Compton sounded horrified.

"No, I hadn't even thought about it."

"Well, you'd darn well better. You never know who's been handing keys around to whom. I hadn't had my first apartment a month when I came home one night to find somebody'd been in, taken a shower, eaten the food I was planning to have for dinner, and walked out wearing the only decent coat I owned. I never did find out who she was, but you can bet your boots I didn't lose any time investing in a new lock; and not the kind that can be opened with a credit card, either. You get hold of a locksmith today, young woman, if you know what's good for you."

Jenny giggled nervously. "Maybe the person who stole your coat sent back the jacket."

"After all these years? Anyway, that was a different place. I suppose it could have been someone who'd seen my address one way or another. He might have happened to visit the apartment building where I'm living now, for instance, and noticed my name on the mailbox, maybe without even being aware of what he was reading. You know how some little thing will stick in your mind for years, for no particular reason. Sending a parcel you wanted to get lost to a place like mine wouldn't be such a bad idea. Our mailman isn't supposed to leave things in the lobby, but he often does. Anyone could have picked it up and said nothing, or the package could have kicked around unclaimed until the janitor either returned it to the post office or threw it out. Then again, as you suggested, the jacket might have been deliberately sent to me."

"But why?"

"Who knows? I've made a surprising number of enemies in my day, Miss Plummer. Lots of embezzlers think it's all the accountant's fault when they get caught and sent to jail. I've had high-powered executives cuss me out in grand style for being a fool woman who didn't know how the game was played, simply because I wouldn't take a fat bribe and cover up for them. I've had anonymous letters and threatening phone calls. Once or twice I've even been in danger of getting beaten up or worse. It wouldn't surprise me if some old acquaintance thought it would be fun to dump incriminating evidence on me and set me up for a murder rap."

Elderly ladies in the Plummer family didn't allude to being set up for murder raps, but Jenny had no doubt Miss Compton was only stating the facts as she saw them.

"Now," the woman went on, "getting back to that return address. There's the chance, you know, that I was meant to find it. Whoever sent the jacket might have wanted me to know where it came from, knowing I'd be nosy enough to come charging up here to Meldrum."

"So they could—get at you?" Jenny gasped.

"It's possible, if I'm in the process of being framed. On

the other hand, I'm wondering whether it mightn't have been something in the nature of a cry for help. Most people never think of accountants as detectives, but in a sense that's what we are. White-collar crime doesn't get into the papers as often as the shoot 'em up on the streets kind, but it's there and don't kid yourself it isn't. And on the books is where it's bound to show up, sooner or later. Our job is spotting it as quickly as possible.

"Exposing fraud has a positive as well as a negative side, you know. When a guilty person is caught, all the innocent ones are off the hook. Saving a firm from being run out of business by being robbed of its assets means saving the jobs of its employees. I've never been afraid to ask questions, and most of my clients have been grateful for my services in tracing defalcations. Some of them have rather exaggerated notions about my knack for nosing out a crook, and they've passed the word around. Say there's someone who knows about me and also knows there's something around here that ought to be exposed. He or she doesn't dare or doesn't choose to get personally involved, so they think up a nice, subtle way of putting the old bloodhound on the trail. That's what I prefer to think, and I suppose it's really why I was willing to stick my neck out by coming to Meldrum. Though I hadn't intended to do more than sniff out the source."

"I can understand your coming," said Jenny. In essence, it was what she herself had done. The difference was that Miss Compton had experience and training, whereas she herself had just taken a flying leap without stopping to think where it might land her.

Could the jacket be her father's? She didn't have the

faintest idea how he'd died, she hadn't even known he was dead until the fantastic news came about all that money. And then she'd been so bowled over by getting it, and so deafened by the Plummers' yammering about where Jason Cirak had accumulated his wealth, that she hadn't pushed as hard as she might have for details of his sudden demise. Was Miss Compton's involvement somehow connected with the devious financial dealings of the man who'd called himself James Cox? Had her father been one of the accountant's grateful clients? Or one of her catches?

"Could you make out the postmark?" she asked cautiously. "Was the package mailed from Meldrum?"

"Oh, no, I can't imagine anyone's being that careless. It was sent from Providence on the fourth of October, five days before I received it. I assume the sender took it to a big post office during a rush hour, so that the clerk who handled it would be too busy to remember who brought it in. That's what I'd have done, anyway."

"So there's no hope of tracing the package through the mails?"

"None whatever, in my opinion. I'd say our only chance is right here in Meldrum. My chance, I mean. Obviously, this couldn't possibly have anything to do with you."

Jenny stared down into the cold dregs of her coffee and shook her head. "To tell you the truth," she said at last, "I don't know whether it does or not."

4 ⚘ ⚘ ⚘

She was not yet ready to give her complete confidence to a stranger, but surely there could be no harm in talking about last night. Jenny told it all, not sparing her embarrassment over the palm-reading episode or the subsequent meeting with Lawrence MacRae in the back yard. Miss Harriet Compton didn't take her eyes off Jenny's face once during the telling. Then she nodded briskly, as though she'd balanced a profit-and-loss statement.

"If you told this Firbelle woman there's danger around her, you were probably right. Intuitive people like yourself often pick up signals without being aware of it. You may have caught a glance, a word, a gesture from somebody in the group that registered on your subconscious mind as being somehow out of key. You may have sensed fear in the person herself, even though she was trying to keep it hidden. I've done the same sort of thing often enough myself. A friend of mine used to say I could smell the books cooking."

She smiled, a bit sadly, Jenny thought. "Do you believe the prowler you saw was MacRae?"

"Of course. I mean, it must have been, mustn't it? Only I did think—" Jenny hesitated.

"Go on. You thought what?"

"Well, I wasn't really sure at first whether it was a man or a woman. And MacRae's rather broad in the shoulders for a—but shapes in the dark are always deceiving, aren't they?"

"Not always. Sometimes the dark blots out details that might otherwise throw you off the track. What occurs to me, Miss Plummer, is that MacRae's behavior toward you was unnecessarily rude. After all, you were in your own yard and he was trespassing. It was none of his business what you were up to. The best reason I can think of for his jumping down your throat the way he did would be to keep you from asking the same question of him. It also served to distract your attention, didn't it? If there was another person around, he or she would have had a chance to slip away while you and MacRae were arguing. I think that chap would bear checking out."

"So do I," said Jenny. "I'm just wondering how to go about it."

"My dear Miss Plummer, you don't think I'm going to let you get involved in my little mystery?"

"But I'm already involved," Jenny protested. "I've stuck my neck out just by moving into this house. And besides, anyone in my backyard is my problem."

Harriet Compton gave her another of those long looks. "If you're waiting for me to say nonsense, my dear, I'm afraid you're in for a long wait. From what you tell me, that MacRae man interpreted your warning to Mrs. Firbelle as something quite different from a psychic hunch; and you can bet there were others at the party who thought the same. Somebody may very well have gotten the idea you know more than you're telling and that you pose a threat to him, or her. I wish I knew whether we have two different tigers by the tails, or if we've both grabbed hold of the same one."

"Since I'm playing my hunches, I'll say it's the same one," said Jenny.

"Then we'll have to pull together, or we'll both get mauled. I think what I'd better do now is find a room here in Meldrum and simply hang around till I get a line on what this mess is all about. If somebody did deliberately send for me, I'll be approached sooner or later." Miss Compton shrugged. "Sooner rather than later, no doubt."

"But you could be making yourself a sitting target!"

"So what? I'm a tough old bird." Miss Compton pushed back from the table and picked up her elegant jacket. "You wouldn't happen to know if there's a decent hotel or tourist home or whatever in the neighborhood?"

"I believe I remember seeing a motel a few miles down on the Providence road," Jenny answered, "but I doubt if you'd accomplish much hanging around out there. What you need is a base of operations right here in the village, and some way of getting to know people without making them suspicious. I think you'd better stay with me."

39

The invitation was out before she'd had time to think it over. Miss Compton smiled and shook her head.

"That's sweet of you, Miss Plummer, but I couldn't barge in on you like that." She started to put on her coat, then stopped with one arm halfway through a sleeve. "What am I talking about? This is hardly the time to stand on ceremony, is it? You're absolutely right, it's the only thing that makes sense. You can introduce me to the locals, and if anybody does start trouble, you'll be a darn sight safer with me in the house than you would be alone. How old are you, anyway?"

"Twenty-four," Jenny lied.

"Oh?" A slight lift of the eyebrow showed Miss Compton hadn't been deceived by a day. "At any rate, once people find out you've taken in a boarder—"

"Oh, I couldn't do that. You'll have to be something else. You see, I'm—well, I have rather a lot of money and I've let my neighbors know it. Jack Firbelle started needling me last night about being a starving author. He got under my skin, so I let him know I wasn't about to starve. I must say he changed his attitude in a hurry. They all did."

"I'll bet. There's nothing more respectable than a fat bank account. All the more reason why you ought to have an old dragon guarding the portcullis. Okay then, I'll be your even richer Aunt Harriet, which means we'll have to go on a shopping spree this afternoon. I didn't even pack a toothbrush because I wasn't planning to do anything more than give somebody an earful and go back to Baltimore. Is there a really good dress shop in the village, do you know?"

"No, but we could go next door and ask the Firbelles. That will give you an excuse to meet them. .We can say you've just got off the plane from Europe and your luggage was hijacked."

"Save it for that book you're supposed to be writing. Never tell any more lies than you have to. I learned that from a very successful embezzler I met once. The closer you stick to the truth, the less apt you are to get caught. I dashed up from Baltimore this morning on the spur of the moment to see your place, found you in a mess, and decided I'd better stay on to help you get settled. What do they call you at home?"

"Jenny. At least that's what I prefer to be called. It's short for Jennifer, and about half the girls I went to school with were named Jennifer."

"Jenny it is, then. You'd better call me Aunt Harriet. Nobody ever has, before. Now you'd better take me out and show me around the place. That's always the first thing you do when you've just bought a home in the suburbs. Where shall I park my hat?"

"You'd better use my room, Aunt Harriet," Jenny replied, trying it on for sound. "There's a sort of guest room, but it's in pretty rough shape at the moment."

"I'll have the guest room. If you're that rich, you don't put yourself out for anybody."

Miss Compton bustled around the tiny spare bedroom, sweeping junk off the dresser top, helping Jenny put fresh linen on the narrow, saggy bed, setting her citified hat on the closet shelf and the gold-mounted attaché case containing the bloodstained jacket on the floor below.

"All moved in. Let's go."

Luck was with them. As they stepped out the back door, they could see Beth Firbelle over near the boundary between the two yards, fussing with some straggly purple chrysanthemums. Jenny led Miss Compton toward her.

"Good morning. Beth Firbelle, I'd like to have you meet my aunt, Miss Harriet Compton. She just breezed in from Baltimore to see how the other half is living."

"And I must say she's not living any too grandly at the moment," Miss Compton put in. "That place is a decorator's nightmare. I'd be glad to stay and pitch in, Jenny, except that I didn't bring any clothes with me."

"That's a lame excuse, coming from you, Aunt Harriet. We'll go buy some. You know how you adore splurging on things you don't need. Beth, is there any place downtown where we could find something for her to wear?"

"Oh, yes, we have lovely shops in Meldrum."

Beth was avidly drinking in every detail of the newcomer's toilette, from the exquisitely carved jade earrings to the sleek-fitting bench-made oxfords. "Aunt Marguerite gets most of her clothes from Louise's Boutique on Main Street."

Jenny was willing to bet the ashes-of-eggplant sweater and skirt Beth was wearing hadn't come from Louise's Boutique. Here, beyond a doubt, was another do-it-yourself project that should never have been done. Beth even had another matching drawstring bag, this one bulging unattractively with shears and garden gloves.

"Come on, Auntie dear," she said. "I'll drive you down to Louise's right this minute. Beth, won't you come along for the ride and show us where it is?"

"I'd love to!" Beth wasn't bad-looking when she smiled.

She was flushed and excited now, looking younger than the forty or so years Jenny had given her last night. "I'll just run in and make sure Aunt Marguerite doesn't want me for anything first. Would you—" She hesitated, obviously wondering whether she dared ask them into the house.

The polite thing would be to murmur, "Go right ahead. We'll just stay here and admire the chrysanthemums," but Jenny realized they weren't going to get anywhere without treading on a few toes. "We'll come with you," she said cheekily. "I want my aunt to meet your aunt."

After that, there was nothing Beth could do but give them a strained little smile and let them come. Jenny could see she was none too happy about letting them in without official permission. As they mounted the longish flight of wooden stairs that led up to the back door, she could feel the tension building at every step.

But why? Was Beth really all that terrified of her aunt? Was it an act of cruelty to force themselves on her like this?

As a former sort of poor relation herself, Jenny could feel a certain kinship with Beth. She didn't recall ever having been afraid of the Plummers, though; mostly frustrated and resentful because they never quit nagging her, trying to force her into becoming something she didn't want to be.

Looking at this dejected creature in the droopy homemade skirt going off to get her aunt, she realized now that things back home could have been a great deal worse. She'd had her own mother with her, for what that was worth. The room they'd shared had been well-furnished and spacious enough for both. It was mainly the lack of privacy Jenny had resented. As to getting along with her mother, that hadn't been any great problem. Marion Plummer had never been unkind or even cross. Whenever Jenny had stepped out of line, as so often happened, she'd simply taken to her bed with a headache and let Aunt Martha do the scolding.

Furthermore, she hadn't actually been a poor relation, even though they'd tried to make her feel like one. Jenny had always known they weren't living on charity because Uncle Fred was too fond of spouting figures at them. He'd kept a special ledger in which he itemized everything from their weekly board and room to Jenny's new tooth-brush, and loved to snap, "Marion, this will have to come out of your next month's share of the interest," whenever either of them spent a penny over their allowances. She'd gotten furious with her mother for sighing, "Please, Fred, you know I have no head for figures. Whatever you do is fine with me." Nobody'd ever asked whether it was all right with Jenny. Even now, she felt a surge of the old fury.

Maybe it was the atmosphere in this house! It struck her as a gloomy place, dark and old and somehow creepy. She was almost shocked when she heard Harriet Compton exclaim, "What a lovely kitchen!"

Jenny looked around then at the room into which Beth had led them. Why hadn't she noticed the graceful tin chandelier hanging from the high ceiling, the round oak table set beside a huge window over which stray tendrils of a grapevine, now touched by frost, showed purple clusters of fruit against silver-bronze leaves? There was a huge black iron stove with polished steel rims around the little shelves that jutted out from its high back and fancy curlicues embossed on its oven doors. A mammoth hutch cabinet was laden with pewter and ironstone. Everything was spotless, gleaming with polish. The walls were painted a warm ivory, the curtains patterned in soft cream and gold. Whatever had made her think it was gloomy?

While Jenny was still trying to sort out her feelings, they heard Marguerite Firbelle's silver tinkle coming through the hall. "Jenny's aunt? How delightful! But you might at least have brought them around the front way, Beth dear."

"And miss seeing this marvelous kitchen?" Harriet Compton was shaking hands, saying all the right things, looking at least as elegant in her tweeds as Mrs. Firbelle in her heather-colored wool dress. Jenny was proud of her, and the neighbor was obviously impressed.

"This is an unexpected pleasure, Miss Compton. My niece tells me you've come to give Jenny a hand getting settled."

"I really came to snoop," the newcomer replied quite honestly. "We have no friends or family in Rhode Island, and I hadn't the faintest idea what Jenny had got herself into. I thought she'd at least choose a place nearer Newport, but I can see now why she picked Meldrum. It's an ideal location for a writer, wouldn't you think?"

"Oh, yes, it couldn't be more suitable," Mrs. Firbelle assured her. "My son has often thought he'd like to write. He was mentioning it at breakfast, as a matter of fact.

Didn't he, Beth? Perhaps you might be willing to give him some pointers on getting started, Jenny."

"I could use a few myself," Jenny confessed, recalling her newly adopted aunt's advice about sticking to the facts as much as possible. "All I've done so far is sit at the typewriter and stare at a blank sheet of paper."

"Jenny has the ability. What she needs is to forget everything else and concentrate on her work," said Harriet Compton with just the right degree of severity. "Not having to get out and scratch for a living is no excuse for her to fritter away her talent, as I've told her time and again."

"You certainly have, Auntie dear." Despite the odd little sensation of disquiet that was still bothering her, Jenny was beginning to enjoy this new role. It was certainly a lot easier to play a part when you had somebody feeding you the perfect line every time.

Mrs. Firbelle tinkled a few more pleasantries, then gave the stamp of approval her own niece had been anxiously waiting for. "But I mustn't keep you here chatting when you have so much to do. Beth tells me you've asked her to show you around our quaint little shops."

"We'd be so glad if she would," said Harriet Compton. "I thought I was just popping up for the day, so I didn't bring anything with me. Then I found Jenny in such a state here that I hadn't the heart to leave, so I've got to pick up some things. What does one need for clothes around here? Can I get by for a few days without a dinner dress?"

Beth leaned forward eagerly, but her aunt only laughed. "Heavens, yes. We're simple folk here in Meldrum."

"All you'll need are a couple of shirtwaisty things and a warm robe to sit around and watch television in," Jenny added. "I don't expect to get invited out, and we can't entertain yet because the house is still a shambles."

If Marguerite Firbelle could ignore a hint the size of that one, she must be thick-skinned as an ox. Not that Jenny wanted to be asked back for a longer visit; in fact she was feeling she couldn't get out of the place fast enough. What was wrong in this charming old house, anyway? Why was she still recalling that little red dot on Marguerite's palm? But was it Mrs. Firbelle herself who was in danger, or was someone else in danger from her? The more she saw of the woman, the less sure Jenny was about how to read that troublesome hunch.

But like it or not, she must push ahead with this new acquaintance. Living so close, the Firbelles must surely have known the man who called himself James Cox. They'd have seen him from these very windows, coming and going through his back door. They must have passed the time of day with him over that little fence between the two yards, perhaps become friendly enough to learn some of the things about him that his daughter so desperately wanted to find out. She made her goodbye as cordial as she could, then led Beth and Harriet down to her brand-new Mustang.

As to entertaining, that might not be such a bad idea. It would be one way to get people talking. After all this airy chat about how rich she was, though, they'd expect her to regale them on caviar and champagne. How did one manage that sort of thing? The Plummers were more the baked beans and boiled dinners type. She'd have to depend on Harriet Compton for pointers.

Backing the shiny little car out of the driveway, Jenny realized she was putting a lot of faith in a total stranger. She had only this woman's own word that the affluence Harriet Compton from Baltimore displayed so discreetly and tastefully came from a successful career as a certified public accountant, or even that the woman was who she said she was. She had only Miss Compton's not very probable story to explain that bloodstained suede jacket now parked beside her spare bed.

She had only her Cirak streak to tell her it was all right to trust Harriet Compton and that she'd better hang onto that feeling because Miss Jennifer Plummer was already in over her head and there was nobody else around here she could depend on to pull her out.

5 ❧❧❧

"What did Mr. Cox die of?"

They were at the Kum-In Kafé, Meldrum's closest approximation to a trendy coffee shop, having a belated lunch. Beth and Jenny sat together on one of the plastic-covered banquettes. Harriet Compton sat facing them, barricaded by bags and boxes.

The shopping trip had been a great success. Beth Firbelle had gained status at the boutique by bringing in two well-heeled new customers, even though she'd bought nothing for herself. Among other things, Jenny had found a simple cocktail dress in an intense shade of coral to replace the purple disaster, just in case they got invited out soon, as she had a strong hunch they would. Harriet Compton had spent well over five hundred dollars in fifteen minutes and been urged with almost tearful fervor by Louise herself to come back soon.

After the orgy at Louise's, Harriet had insisted on making a tour of all the local shops and buying her alleged niece any number of housewarming presents. Jenny had decided she ought to accept them without any fuss. This was the sort of thing a rich aunt would do, and Harriet was obviously having fun doing it.

Jenny hadn't realized what a superb actress she could be. It must be because she had such wonderful support. Harriet Compton was so convincing she was almost scary. Jenny said so, in a whisper, after Beth had excused herself to visit what she'd demurely referred to as the little girls' room.

"I ought to be good," Harriet had replied with a grim chuckle. "I've had to do enough of it in my day. Now it looks to me as if we've got Beth nicely primed for a spot of pumping, don't you think? All we have to do is keep her away from Aunt Marguerite awhile longer."

Hence the prolonged luncheon at the Kum-In Kafé. Beth was thrilled to be treated and only too willing to tell these exciting new acquaintances anything they wanted to know. They worked their way through the neighborhood for a while, then Jenny, trying to get Beth into a really beneficent mood said, "That's a lovely pin you're wearing, Beth."

It was. Beth had put it on her droopy old dress when they'd stopped at the house for Marguerite's blessing on the jaunt. Evidently it was her one dress-up item.

Beth beamed, but as Jenny bent forward as if to touch it, Beth pulled back. "It's mine," she said stiffly.

Poor thing. Beth must be afraid her one lovely object would be taken from her. Jenny quickly changed the subject, moving on to what they were really curious about.

"What do you know about my carriage house?" she asked.

"Yes, who occupied the carriage house before my niece bought it?" Miss Compton asked. "What became of him, or her?"

"It was a him, Mr. Cox. His first name was James. He was the most marvelous neighbor!"

"What about his wife?"

"He was a widower, just about Aunt Marguerite's age, I think. They—I mean all of us—were great friends. Honestly, listening to him talk was better than a movie. He was the most fascinating man I ever met."

She probably hadn't met many, was Jenny's cynical thought. Of course Beth had been bowled over by the famous Jason Cirak charm. So had Marion Plummer, and she'd been loudly lamenting the fact for years.

According to Beth, Mr. Cox had given them nothing to lament about, however. He'd entertained them at the most delightful little dinners, just herself and Jack and Aunt Marguerite. Gourmet cooking was one of his hobbies, it appeared. Beth had thought it funny to see a man being handy around the kitchen. Jack couldn't even boil himself an egg.

Miss Compton wasn't interested in eggs. "If Mr. Cox was fitting so well into the life here in Meldrum, why did he leave?"

For the first time, Beth hesitated and looked unhappy at having to answer. "He didn't leave. He—well, he died."

"What did he die of?"

Now Beth was really upset. "I don't quite know how to tell you."

"Why not?" Miss Compton insisted. "We're bound to hear it from somebody."

"Yes, that's true." Still Beth hesitated, fiddling with the edge of the napkin she'd laid neatly back on the table after she'd finished her meal. "As a matter of fact, nobody is quite sure."

"How remarkable. Do go on."

"All I can say is that Jack and I found him lying dead one morning at the foot of his own back steps. We'd all three planned to go for an early bird walk. Jack's terribly interested in birds, you know. Or if you don't, you soon will. Anyway, he'd been trying to get Mr. Cox—that is, Mr. Cox was getting quite interested, too. So we went over about half-past five, I think it was, to call for him, and there he was. Jack was dreadfully upset." Evidently Beth felt her own feelings weren't worth commenting on.

"I can imagine," said Miss Compton. "What did you do?"

"We didn't know what to do. There was blood all over his face. We thought at first he might have tripped and banged his face and got a nosebleed or something as he was coming out to meet us. So we tried to help him up and started asking him if he was all right and that sort of thing, you know. But he was all stiff and cold, so then we knew. Jack got sick to his stomach and couldn't bear to look any more, so it turned out I had to stay with Mr. Cox while Jack ran home and called Dr. Olken. And

Dr. Olken told him to call the police, so of course he had to. That upset Aunt Marguerite dreadfully."

"I can imagine," murmured Miss Compton. "What did the police say?"

"They didn't know what to make of it any more than we did. They got cross because we'd moved him and kept asking us stupid questions about what position he'd been in when we found him and things like that. We told them he simply looked as if he'd fallen down the steps. I mean, what else could you say?"

"But there are only three little steps, and nothing but dirt underneath," Jenny protested. "How could a man be killed by such a short fall?"

"That's what nobody could understand. It did seem odd, but the ground was still frozen hard and, as Jack said, you can't argue with cold facts. Everybody thought a burglar must have got in and hit him over the head while he was trying to get away or something; but as far as anybody could tell, nothing had been taken. His wallet was in his pocket, and it had over two hundred dollars in it."

Beth mentioned the sum with something like reverence. "And the television set and so forth were still in the house, all the stuff burglars usually take, you know. Of course, some people started a rumor that he must have had a lot of valuables hidden away and that was what had been taken; but how could you tell? His cleaning woman was the only person around here who could have known, and she wouldn't have gone prowling through his private belongings, no matter what anybody says. Poor Marie's been the loser, if you ask me. She used to do housework for quite a few different families around town, but nobody will hire her any more. She was living on welfare the last I heard."

"But that's awful!" Jenny was more shocked by the injustice done this unknown Marie than by the horrible way her father had died. She forgot for the moment that he'd thought of her in the end and remembered only the years of misery at the Plummers' when she'd been the child of a runaway father and an ever-complaining deserted wife. Obviously by his death, Jason Cirak had left yet another woman to suffer the consequences.

"And they've still not found out what happened?" Harriet Compton pressed.

"No, never. The coroner's inquest brought in a verdict of death by misadventure, with insufficient evidence to show cause. They couldn't even say for sure whether it was the injury to the front of his head or the loss of blood or the shock and exposure that he actually died from. His nose had been broken and there was a big bang on his forehead, but the skull wasn't fractured. They figured he'd been knocked unconscious and lain there bleeding from the broken nose till the cold got him, or something. I couldn't follow all the medical testimony. Anyway, it had happened the night before instead of in the morning, because they decided he must have been dead quite a while before Jack and I found him. At least five or six hours, they thought. They couldn't say for sure. It had been down below freezing that night."

"When did it happen?"

"Early this past March. The fifth, I think it was."

"The fifth of March?" said Miss Compton sharply. "I thought you said you were going for a bird walk."

"We were. There are lots of birds around in March. Nuthatches, titmice, white-throated sparrows. . . ." Beth's voice trailed off, then she pulled herself together. "Well, this is hardly the sort of conversation for the luncheon table. I hope I haven't put you off your new house, Jenny."

"Oh, no. It's nothing to do with me," Jenny replied with her mouth so dry she could barely get the words out.

Miss Compton wasn't making any pretence of being easy in her mind about the incident. "I don't like this at all, Jenny. If this is the sort of neighborhood you've moved into—"

"It's not the neighborhood," Beth protested. "Aunt Marguerite's lived here all her life and nothing like this has ever happened before. That's why we're all so sure it must have been some kind of freak accident. He must have hit his face on the steps when he fell, or—"

"Do you honestly think that, or do you only want to?"

"Why certainly we want to. The—the alternative would be—" Again Beth didn't complete her sentence.

"Murder, you mean." No euphemisms for Harriet Compton. "So I suppose the property owners in Meldrum put pressure on the local authorities to pass it off as misadventure and hush up the talk as quickly as possible."

She started gathering up her purchases. "I daresay I'd have done the same if I'd been living in Meldrum at the time. That sort of thing doesn't help real-estate values. Here, Jenny, you take this box."

Jenny was aghast at the apparent callousness of Harriet Compton's remark. Beth, however, nodded eager agreement.

"That's what everybody was saying."

Jenny tried to keep her face and voice calm. "Were Mr. Cox's relatives satisfied with the verdict?"

"He didn't have any. I understand all his money went to some charitable foundation none of us had ever heard of before. It does seem an awful shame when I think of how he and Aunt Marguerite—" Beth flushed and stopped short.

Miss Compton pounced. "You mean there was a little romance brewing?"

"Jack and I thought so. It would have been so wonderful for both of them. Aunt Marguerite's been a widow ever since Jack was twelve."

"What did the rest of the family think about your aunt's remarrying? Not that it's any business of mine, of course," Miss Compton added out of politeness.

"Oh, but it's so nice to talk to somebody who *listens!*" Probably not many did, to Beth. "I can't say Pamela and Greg were overly pleased with the idea. Greg took a dislike to Mr. Cox right away. I don't know why, unless it was because he felt slighted. Mr. Cox didn't invite him to dinner, the way he did us. Greg always has to be the center of attention. You must have noticed that at the Gileses', Jenny."

"He did seem to want to be noticed," Jenny agreed, thinking of those hairy, sweaty, grabby paws she'd had so much trouble ducking.

"I suppose Greg had visions of a horde of unexpected Coxes turning up after the wedding and latching onto your aunt's money," said Harriet Compton, who obviously didn't believe in beating around bushes. "Some people's minds always seem to run in that direction."

"Greg Bauer's does, no doubt about that." Beth sniffed. "If there's a dollar floating around, you can bet Greg's will be the first hand stretched out after it. Some of the things he's said about me personally—well, you don't want to hear about that."

Beth slung the drawstring of her hideous crocheted bag over her arm. "I'm sorry. I didn't mean to bore you with family gossip. It's just that I so seldom get a chance to say what I think. Naturally I can't complain to Jack or Aunt Marguerite, and I wouldn't dare breathe a word to any of the neighbors. You being outsiders—oh dear, that doesn't sound very nice."

"Why not? It's what we are," Harriet Compton reassured her. "Jenny and I aren't connected to anybody in Meldrum except each other, so you're free to say what you please without being afraid it will bounce back in your face."

Beth smiled, showing teeth that ought to have been straightened when she was a child, then closed her unlipsticked mouth as if she'd been caught doing something wicked. "You're so kind. Please let me carry some of those parcels for you. And you will forget what I said about James Cox, I hope?"

"Don't worry," said Harriet Compton.

Jenny nodded. Why should Beth worry? Jenny herself would be doing enough worrying for all three of them.

6

However grim the errand that had brought Harriet Compton to the carriage house, Jenny was glad to have her. Harriet was in the tiny kitchen now, putting away a staggering heap of groceries she'd insisted on buying. She'd chased Jenny out to rake leaves because it was such a glorious fall day and young people were better out than in.

"Hi! Working hard?" The voice was Sue Giles's.

Actually, Jenny had been thoroughly enjoying herself and hated to quit for a chat with her neighbor. She tried not to look annoyed as she walked over to the hedge that separated her yard from the Gileses'.

"No, I'm just trying to tidy the place up a little. I meant to call you later on, to thank you for inviting me to your lovely party."

That was a flat lie. Jenny had completely forgotten, which was understandable, all things considered, but hardly excusable. Plummers were punctilious about things like that even if Ciraks weren't, and she'd been brought up to mind her manners.

Sue was quite ready to forgive her. "I'm the one who should be thanking you. You were the hit of the evening. People have been on the phone all day, talking about you. We had no idea you were a lady of so many talents."

"Oh, you mean the palm-reading act?" Jenny turned red. "I only did it for fun. It's a way of getting to know people." She was going to add, "I hope nobody took me seriously," when she recalled that most of them had, Sue included.

"Honestly, I don't see how you could know all that stuff about perfect strangers. You sure hit the nail on the head with Greg Bauer, I want to tell you. And when you told Marguerite Firbelle she'd better watch her step, I almost dropped the cold cuts. If you want my candid opinion, that was another bull's-eye."

Sue laughed, but her shrewish little eyes never shifted from Jenny's face. Jenny didn't know what to reply, so she just looked interested and kept quiet. That was all Sue needed. She leaned over the hedge and lowered her voice to the confidential, insistent murmur of the well-practiced scandalmonger.

"I'd be the last person in the world to say anything, but if I were in Marguerite Firbelle's shoes, I wouldn't feel too safe, either. When you consider some of the people she's got hanging around her—"

Jenny didn't like this a bit. "But I didn't say she was in

danger from a person. She could slip in the bathtub, or get an allergic bee sting."

"Sure, she could. Or fall down three little steps and break her neck. Or get her head bashed in by a burglar the police never found any sign of."

Now it was making sense. Sue wasn't just muckraking, she was scared. Living so close to the carriage house, maybe she had a reason. Jenny said what she had to.

"You're talking about Mr. Cox, aren't you?"

Sue blinked. "Oh, so you've heard about him already. Who told you?"

There wasn't much point in trying to cover up. No doubt half of Meldrum already knew about that shopping expedition and the cozy lunch at the Kum-In Kafé.

"It was Beth Firbelle."

"You don't say! I didn't realize you and Beth were so friendly."

"She seems very pleasant," Jenny replied rather angrily. Why shouldn't poor relations have friends? She felt an urge to stick up for Beth, but it would be stupid to make an enemy of Sue.

"My aunt and I kidnapped her," she explained. "You haven't met my aunt, Harriet Compton, yet, but you will. She flew in this morning unannounced, to see what I was up to. When she saw the state my house is in, she decided to stay and help me get things under control. Aunt Harriet hadn't brought any clothes with her, so when we happened to see Beth out in her yard, we asked if she'd come for a ride with us and show us where the shops were. Then we had lunch, and Aunt Harriet got to asking her questions about the neighborhood. You know what older women are like. Naturally we were both interested in knowing who'd had the carriage house before me, and that's how we found out about Mr. Cox."

"I'm surprised Beth could bring herself to tell you," Sue answered. "I'd have thought she'd be the last person."

"I know, having found the body and all. She wasn't any too keen on talking about it, but we rather pushed her, I'm afraid. Anyway, we were bound to hear it from somebody sooner or later."

"So Beth figured she might as well make sure you got the official version. She's not as dumb as she looks, you know. I don't suppose she happened to mention that there'd been a marriage in the offing, did she?"

"She didn't say that, no. She did say they'd been friendly with him."

"Um-h'm. Well, at least now the Firbelles don't have to worry any more about the money going out of the family."

"But Mr. Cox wouldn't have been after money. He was a rich man himself," Jenny protested. "I mean, Beth gave me the impression he was."

Sue Giles shrugged. "You couldn't prove it by me. They say he entertained quite lavishly. Bill and I never got a chance to find out."

Was Sue just being catty because Cox had snubbed her and her husband, or did she in fact know something? Jenny decided she'd better not try to handle this alone.

"Speaking of entertaining, Sue, could I lure you in for a cup of tea right now? We've just been laying in supplies, and I'd love to have you meet my aunt."

"I really shouldn't. I'm such a mess." Sue made fluttering gestures at her disheveled hair and rumpled pants, but was through the hedge before she'd finished explaining why she couldn't come.

Miss Compton was delighted to meet Mrs. Giles. Mrs. Giles was obviously impressed by Miss Compton. Jenny was pleased with herself for having trapped another potential source of information.

"You two stay here and get acquainted while I make the tea. Do you prefer cream or lemon, Sue?"

"Plain milk, please, if you have it."

"Of course."

As Jenny turned to go out to the kitchen, though, she caught a rueful glance from Harriet Compton. What was that supposed to mean? Then she remembered her new aunt had been putting away the groceries just now. Could they possibly have forgotten to buy something so basic as milk?

A glance into the refrigerator showed her they could, and had. Now what? Go back and confess? She guessed what Sue would say to that, as soon as she found a willing ear to say it into: "Oh, sure, they put on a big front, but they didn't even have enough milk in the house for a cup of tea. There's something funny about that pair, you mark my words."

She put on the kettle to boil, picked up a small pitcher, and sped up the knoll to the Firbelles' house, hoping to find Beth alone in the kitchen. No such luck. She could hear voices through an open window, and neither was Beth's. What of it? They were neighbors, weren't they? And Beth could testify she was no cheapskate, even if she did have to borrow half a cupful of milk in an emergency.

She had one foot on the bottom step when something she heard from above made her stop short.

"Mother, I'm begging you one last time. We can't let this go on any longer. The risk—"

"Jack, you know the situation as well as I. I accept the risk, unless you accept the alternative. We shan't discuss it any more."

After that, all Jenny heard was the unmistakable bang of a door being slammed. She might as well go up and ask for the milk.

She raced up the stairs making as much noise as she could, so they wouldn't think she'd been hanging around overhearing what they'd said. Now she knew she hadn't imagined the feeling of tension in this house. Risk, Jack had said, and he'd sounded distraught. Marguerite Firbelle, on the other hand, answered Jenny's knock looking calm and collected as usual.

"Why, Jenny. What can I do for you?"

"I'm sorry to be a pest, Mrs. Firbelle, but Sue Giles just dropped in for a cup of tea and would you believe that with all that enormous shopping we did today, we completely forgot to buy milk? Could you possibly spare just a drop?"

"Certainly. Won't you come in?"

"Thanks, but I mustn't. I've put the kettle on, and they don't even know I'm not there to rescue it. When I realized about the milk, I just grabbed the pitcher and rushed madly over here. Now I've got to rush madly back."

"Then I mustn't keep you, must I?"

Marguerite Firbelle took the pitcher into the house.

She seemed mildly amused. Or was it relief that was causing those well-controlled features to relax a bit? Jenny had no time to wonder. She accepted the half-filled pitcher when the woman brought it back, burbled her thanks, and hurried home, knowing Mrs. Firbelle and perhaps Jack also would be watching to make sure she did.

Harriet and Sue hadn't missed her. The ripple of voices from the living room told her they were getting along just fine. She needn't break her neck hurrying with the tea. That was a lucky break. Jenny needed time to catch her breath and sort out her thoughts.

Beth's account of how her father died had shaken her badly, and there was no sense in trying to pretend it hadn't. Those remarks of Sue Giles's a few minutes ago hadn't made her feel any better. And that risk Jack Firbelle was so uptight about, was it something that affected just him and his mother, or did it involve the whole village?

What was going on in this supposedly humdrum little place? Was Jason Cirak killed simply because he'd had the bad luck to move into the wrong house? Was that bloodstained jacket, mailed to Harriet Compton from this address so long after he'd been found right outside that back door with his skull bashed in, somehow involved with his mysterious death? Or did it mean there'd been another murder, one that nobody even knew about yet?

"How's the tea doing, Jenny? Want some help?"

Harriet Compton's voice jolted her back to the business at hand. She called back, "Just coming," and picked up the tray she'd been absent-mindedly getting ready while she pondered.

Jack Firbelle was the man on the pan when she carried it into the living room. "He's never done a tap of work that I know of," Sue was informing Harriet. "He passed the bar after he finished law school, but he's never gone into practice. He's supposed to have a weak heart, but I notice it never keeps him from doing anything he wants to."

"Beth seems willing to earn her keep, anyway," Jenny ventured. "She was out working in the garden this morning."

Sue shook her head. "Oh, Beth's willing enough, I guess. Has to be, in her circumstances. I don't know why her aunt lets her go around looking like a walking ragbag the way she does."

"Has Beth always lived with Mrs. Firbelle?"

"No, only for the past five years or so. She arrived one day in a taxi with a bunch of junk, and there she's stayed. If you ask me, Jack's hanging on to her so she'll be there to keep house for him when Aunt Marguerite goes. Then there won't be any excuse for Pam and Greg to move in. Greg thought he was doing a big thing for himself when he waltzed Pam Firbelle to the altar, but he's had a rude awakening, I can tell you that. Old Maggie's a lot tighter with a dollar than he expected her to be, and Jack's not going to be any different when his turn comes."

Jenny began to wonder if Sue Giles had had an eye on either Jack or Greg before she married Bill. She wasn't a bad-looking woman and she couldn't be much over forty, if that. Bill Giles must be at least fifteen years older than she, a quiet man with a middle-aged spread, who didn't look as if he'd be an exciting husband. If it wasn't a disappointing marriage, then what had planted all these sour grapes in Sue's personal vineyard? Was she this catty about everybody in Meldrum? If so, how could she be such a popular hostess? Both Greg and Jack had been wading into the goodies last night as eagerly as the rest of the crowd and not being stingy with the compliments to the cook, either.

It must be this clan loyalty thing, Jenny decided. The Plummers were like that. They were always ripping each other up the back among themselves, but let a stranger attack one of them and the rest would leap at his throat. People's foibles could be endured as long as they belonged. Her father hadn't belonged to the Plummers, so they'd cast him to outer darkness. He hadn't belonged to Meldrum, so he'd been murdered. She didn't belong, either, and she'd better keep that fact in mind.

"The Firbelles must be a good-sized family," she remarked as she passed Sue a plate of pastries from the bake shop they'd stopped at with Beth. "I met one of the cousins, Daisy Green, I believe her name was. She was telling me who was related to whom at your party. Too bad you missed it, Aunt Harriet," she threw in as cream for the cat. "Sue is the most marvelous hostess. You never saw such food, and I'm sure I met everybody worth knowing in Meldrum."

Plus a number who weren't, judging from the earful Sue had just been giving them. "There were so many I got confused after a while. Who was that man with the red mustache, Sue? Is he another Firbelle?"

Mrs. Giles put down the silver teaspoon she'd been furtively examining to see whether it was sterling or only plated and gave Jenny the speculative glance she'd anticipated. "Larry MacRae? Perish the thought! His grandmother would have a Scotch conniption if she ever heard you say a thing like that. She and Marguerite Firbelle have carried on a running feud for the past thirty years."

"What about?"

"Don't ask me. It's been going on so long, I doubt if they remember themselves. Too bad old Elspeth couldn't make it last night. You'd have got a kick out of watching her and Marguerite high-hat each other."

Harriet Compton raised her eyebrows. "Do you mean people actually invite them both to the same affairs?"

Sue laughed. "You have to. If I'd slighted either one, they'd both be down on me. Social life in Meldrum is more complicated than you might think."

"You'll have to teach me the ropes," said Jenny, wondering how she could get back to Lawrence MacRae without causing further complications. "So the grandmother is Elspeth MacRae?"

"No, Elspeth Gillespie."

"Gillespie? Is that a Scotch name?"

"Is it ever! She's even got a Gillespie tartan collar for her cat."

"She sounds as if she'd be fun to meet," said Harriet Compton. "Can't you invite her over tomorrow, Jenny?"

"I don't see how. I haven't met her myself, just the grandson, and I don't think he even likes me."

Sue Giles pricked up her ears. "What makes you say that?"

Good question. How was one supposed to answer that? "Well, he didn't act any too friendly. He wouldn't let me read his palm, for one thing."

"Probably afraid you'd see what it is he does on those business trips he's always taking. Larry's kind of a dark horse, if you ask me. Disappears for weeks on end and claims he's been off on assignment. He makes good money, they say, and Elspeth's always bragging about what a great photographer he is, but I sure wouldn't want any grandson of mine chasing after those sexy models."

"Is that what he does, fashion photography?"

"I couldn't say. All I can tell you is Larry MacRae doesn't waste much time cooling his heels in Meldrum."

Evidently that really was all Sue Giles could say, or at least all she had time for. It was almost five o'clock, and Bill was a man who expected his dinner to be ready when he got home from work. Sue wiggled her way back through the hedge, leaving Jenny and Harriet free to assess what she'd said.

"Did that get us anywhere?" Jenny asked.

Harriet shrugged and began gathering up the tea things. "We'd already learned from Beth Firbelle that there's an unexplained death connected with this house. Now Sue tells us the dead man was supposed to have been going to marry Mrs. Firbelle, who's not only rich but also related to half the village. She says Larry Mac-Rae's always taking mysterious trips and that his grandmother, Mrs. Gillespie, doesn't like Mrs. Firbelle. It hardly seems likely MacRae and his grandmother would bump off that poor Mr. Cox just to spite his fiancée, but you never know. Sue also says Jack Firbelle's real illness is an allergy to work, and that his brother-in-law, Greg Bauer, is beginning to think he made a bad bargain when he married Pamela."

"Sounds like a plot for a soap opera," said Jenny. "Was Greg afraid he'd lose his chance of an inheritance from his mother-in-law if she remarried? Assuming Sue Giles is right and M-Mr. Cox really intended to marry Mrs. Firbelle, which I don't believe for one minute."

"Why not?" Harriet wanted to know.

Jenny could have told her because it would have been too much like getting stuck with the Plummer tribe again, but she wasn't ready to do that. "Because he had such a wild taste in slipcovers, I suppose," she hedged. "It just doesn't feel right to me. Of course, even if he didn't, but the Firbelles thought he did, they'd still be scared, wouldn't they? Pamela might have been worried that her own marriage might go down the tube if Greg got too uptight about the money. And Beth could have figured she'd be out of a home because her aunt's new husband wouldn't want poor relations camped on the premises."

"And there may be any number of things we don't know about yet, so let's not start jumping to conclusions," said Harriet Compton.

"I wish there were some way of finding out what Mr. Cox's blood type was," Jenny mused. "Then we could find out if it matched the stains on that suede jacket."

Harriet didn't make any reply for a little while, then she nodded. "I knew you'd turn out to be intelligent. What else do your hunches tell you?"

"That I'm in big trouble," Jason Cirak's daughter answered frankly. "I wish I'd never come here!"

Tea tray in hand, the older woman stood looking down at the white-faced young woman hunched on the edge of the garish sofa with her fists clenched and her too-fancy wig askew.

"Jenny, there's something you haven't told me, isn't there?"

"Yes."

"Do you want to tell me now?"

"No."

If Harriet Compton was offended by the curt monosyllables, she showed no sign. "That's right, my dear. Never trust anybody until you're sure."

"I trust you. I just don't know what to say."

Jenny pulled off the hot wig and sat looking down at the tangle of black acrylic curls as though trying to remember how the thing had got into her hand. "I'm beginning to realize that I've made a big mistake, and I'm scared. I'm even more scared than Sue Giles."

"Sue Giles?" Harriet Compton was startled. "How do you know that? She didn't act scared."

"Well, she is. Don't ask me how I know. I feel it, that's all. It's like last night with Mrs. Firbelle. I felt it, and I said it!"

She was almost screaming, her voice beginning to shake.

"Jenny, stop that!" Harriet's matter-of-fact voice cut into the mounting hysteria. "Listen to me, Jenny. How old are you?"

"I'll be nineteen next week." She was too exhausted to lie any more.

"And this is your first time away from home, right?"

"I never had a home. My mother and I always lived with Uncle Fred and Aunt Martha Plummer."

"Why? What happened to your father?"

"You tell me." Jenny had no defenses left now. "That's what I came here to find out."

"Your father was James Cox."

"My father was—yes, my father was James Cox. And he left me all his money even though I hadn't seen him since I was a baby. And I got sick of listening to the Plummers nagging and nattering and grinding their teeth over the money and where it came from, so I came charging down here like the heroine of some idiotic paperback novel to s-solve—"

Harriet Compton sat down on the sofa and slipped an inexpressibly comforting arm around the dead man's trembling daughter.

"You poor, poor kid! Listen to me, Jenny. There's nothing abnormal about extrasensory perception. Everybody has it, to a greater or lesser degree. You happen to be more sensitive than the average, that's all. Look at it positively. Being able to tune in on other people's feelings may be uncomfortable sometimes, but it's also a protection for you. Can't you see that?"

"I suppose so. Thanks, Aunt Harriet."

Jenny still didn't move, not wanting to draw away from the reassuring pressure of the older woman's arm, not feeling secure enough to lean closer. "You know, you said this morning that suede jacket might have been a cry for help. This is another crazy idea, but—do you think it's possible I'm the person you were brought here to help?"

The elderly accountant cleared her throat, as though

some word she didn't want to say had got caught there. "That's not such a crazy idea, Jenny. Maybe it was and maybe it wasn't, but you need somebody, and I'm here. That's what matters, isn't it?"

7

Aunt Harriet—Jenny was beginning to forget she wasn't actually related to this visitor of a day—turned on James Cox's record player while they ate dinner. Jenny was half amused, half appalled to learn that the father she'd always pictured as a suave cosmopolite had been a country and western addict. Nevertheless, steak, salad, and "I've Got Tears in My Ears Lying Flat on My Back in Bed Cryin' over You" were effective therapy.

"Here's one for you, Jenny." Miss Compton was having a marvelous time reading titles. " 'You Stepped on the Corns of My Heart.' Or how about 'Does the Spearmint Lose Its Flavor on the Bedpost Overnight?' That was one of the great joys of my childhood. I think your father must have acquired these records along with the house."

She talked of James Cox as a real human being who'd

lived in this house, eaten at this table; not as a legendary
character who'd come to a bad end as Uncle Fred had always said he would. Jenny found it an intense relief, being able to picture Jason Cirak doing small, unimportant
things. Not flouting convention, not dodging responsibility, not breaking anybody's heart or borrowing anybody's money, just sitting in one of these lumpy, gaudy
armchairs listening to some bugle-nosed rhinestone cow-
boy wailing about the lone prairie and the perfidy of
woman.

He hadn't been a young man when he married Marion
Plummer. So he must have been quite old by the time he
died. He'd probably had backaches and sore feet and false
teeth that got seeds under them when he tried to eat rasp-
berry jam. It must be tough to be a gone-to-seed Lothario,
finding yourself alone when you couldn't go a-wooing
any longer and needed somebody to bring you a cup of
tea in bed when your rheumatics were acting up. Maybe
he was sorry his marriage had gone sour, sorrier than
Marion Plummer for all her weeping and wailing. Maybe
that was why he'd been playing around with the idea of
marrying Mrs. Firbelle, if it was true that he had.

Yet surely he hadn't meant to commit bigamy. Would
he have asked her mother again for a divorce, after all
these years? Or was he merely having one last fling with
a good-looking woman and had he carried the game a
step too far?

Did his death have anything to do with Marguerite
Firbelle at all? As the family kept reminding her, there
was all that money, and he hadn't gotten it making

movies nobody wanted to see. It must have come from somewhere.

Why hadn't she told Harriet Compton the whole story? Why hadn't she explained that James Cox was Jason Cirak, who'd lived poor and died rich? If this strange woman was willing to help, didn't she deserve all the facts, or at least all Jenny knew?

It wasn't the right time to tell.

No, that wasn't true. Now was as good a time as any. Jenny simply wasn't ready to share Jason Cirak with anybody. She'd been without a father almost all her life. Only since she'd come here had she begun to experience him as somebody who'd lived, not in a few old photographs but in the flesh, someone to whom she owed her being, someone who'd pretended not to care about her but had spent years amassing a fortune to leave her. She wanted to keep him with her for a little while before she let anybody take him away from her again.

Harriet Compton wouldn't hurt her deliberately. Jenny was sure of that. There was a good deal about the woman that puzzled her, something strong that she could feel but not understand, but mostly there was goodness. It wasn't the Fred Plummer kind of goodness, the kind that warned you not to get caught doing anything someone could sue you for. It wasn't Aunt Martha's brand of sweetness and light, giving you a headache so she could flutter around you with aspirin and cologne when all you wanted was a chance to call your soul your own. Harriet Compton's version of the Golden Rule probably read "Do your enemies before they do you." Nevertheless she was good.

Jenny could feel it, a wiry, workaday kind of decency

that wouldn't turn squashy and start dishing out plati-
tudes in a pinch. She'd waste no time wringing her hands,
but would get in there shoulder-to-shoulder with you and
do whatever had to be done. It was silly to think some unknown friend had sent the retired accountant to fish Jenny
Cirak out of the mess she'd so blindly hurled herself into,
but it was an indescribable relief to have Harriet Compton with her now.

All right, so she had been crazy to come to Meldrum.
Would she have been any saner to stay with the Plummers? Mother was never going to forgive Jenny for having been the one to inherit Jason Cirak's money. Uncle
Fred, Aunt Martha, and the rest of the tribe would never
quit harping about ingratitude, even if Jenny were to
turn every penny over to them. How long would she have
been able to endure their snide guesses about how that
wastrel Jason had managed to pick so much cabbage?
How many more times would she have had to catch side-
long looks and portentous remarks about "Blood will
tell," every time she got within twenty feet of an eligible
man?

It must have been downright ghastly for a man with
such uninhibited tastes in music and chintzes to find out
he'd married the whole Plummer clan instead of just
pretty, clingy Marion. Maybe Jason Cirak had been trying to provide himself with respectable connections, as
Aunt Martha so loudly maintained, but he couldn't have
realized how devastating all that concentrated respecta-
bility was going to be until he was stuck with it. Poor
Father! Jenny was beginning to feel a kinship with him,
reprobate though he no doubt was.

"Company's coming." Harriet Compton must have sharp ears. Even over the blare of the phonograph, she'd heard footsteps coming up the walk moments before the front doorbell rang. "Watch it, Jenny. Don't open the door till you find out who it is."

She hovered like a bodyguard while Jenny called out, "Who's there?"

The answer came low and urgent. "Greg Bauer. Can I see you for a minute? It's important."

"That's Mrs. Firbelle's son-in-law," Jenny whispered. "What shall I do?"

"Let him in. I'll be in the kitchen. Find out what he's after."

"I know darn well what he's after," Jenny muttered cynically, but she was wrong. Greg Bauer wasn't grabbing tonight.

"Look, Jenny, can you do me a big favor?"

"That depends on what it is," she replied.

"Can you—" He took a deep breath and thrust out his hand. "Can you see anything there about Peruvians Unlimited?"

"About what?" Jenny gaped open-mouthed at the sweating palm. "Of course, I can't. I don't even know what you're talking about."

"Well, do you see a big killing?"

"He means on the stock market, Jenny." Harriet Compton's voice came, deep and amused, out of the dark. "I'd stay far, far away from Peruvians, young man. In my opinion, Consolidated Federal is a much better risk."

"What risk? Con Fed hasn't moved a point in six months."

"There's a rumor around that in about three weeks it's going to announce a jump in profits and a split in shares. If you keep your mouth shut and pick up what you can now, you won't need a fortune-teller to make you a killing."

"On the level?" Greg Bauer was still holding out his hand but he'd forgotten Jenny was even there. "Can I count on that?"

"As much as you can count on anything in the stock market. Just don't go repeating what I said and jacking up the price. If your broker asks you why you want a dog like Con Fed, tell him you're interested in a safe long-term investment and he'll tell you you're nuts, but never mind. Once it splits, watch till it starts to level off, then take your profit, shove most of it in a high-interest savings account, and if you still feel like sticking your neck out, buy a few shares of Peruvian just for kicks. Never speculate with money you can't afford to lose, young man, and never, never gamble with anybody's money but your own. There aren't all that many successful embezzlers around, and you don't look to me as if you have the brains to be one of them."

"Say, who are you, anyway?"

"This is my aunt, Harriet Compton." Jenny was enjoying herself now. "And you'd better believe she knows what she's talking about. Greg Bauer is the husband of Beth Firbelle's cousin Pamela, Aunt Harriet."

"How do you do, Mr. Bauer," said Miss Compton. "So that's why you're anxious to get rich quick."

"Are you a witch or something?" he gasped.

"I've been called that, among other things. Here, Mr.

Bauer, let me take your jacket. Jenny, is there any coffee left?"

"I'll get some."

Jenny fled to the kitchen where she could have her laugh unseen. Harriet Compton in action was really something. A rabbit being hypnotized by a rattlesnake, if such things actually did happen, would probably wear much the same expression as the one on Greg Bauer's handsome, puffy face right now.

When she came back in with the warmed-over coffee, three mugs, and some cream and sugar, she found the victim wedged helplessly into a corner of the sofa. The accountant was giving him a stern lecture on the intricacies of finance while the phonograph blatted, "You're Sweet an' Petite but I'm Seven Foot Two, So I Gotta Find Me More Woman Than You."

Bauer drank his coffee like a shellshock victim, then struggled out of the sofa and said he had to be getting along. Mercifully, Harriet Compton let him go.

"I've enjoyed meeting you, Mr. Bauer. Do let me know how you make out with Con Fed."

"I'll get your jacket," Jenny said quickly. She rummaged in the closet. "Let me help you."

"Hey, this can't be mine."

Greg Bauer had to be telling the truth. The suede jacket Jenny was holding for him would never have covered those wide shoulders with their extra padding of fat.

"Oh, sorry," she apologized with a straight face. "This must be the one I found hanging in the closet when I moved here. It must have belonged to that Mr. Cox who lived here before I did. You don't happen to recall seeing it on him?"

"No, I can't say I do."

Greg was fingering the rich-textured suede, perhaps wishing he could have laid claim to the garment. "It's a beautiful jacket, but it doesn't look like Cox, somehow. He either went in for the wildest plaids you ever saw or else he'd get all togged out in dark gray pinstripes and a black homburg like a London banker. We used to get a kick out of his clothes because they always went from one extreme to the other."

"I see," said Miss Compton. "This jacket is too middle-of-the-road. Mr. Cox must have been an interesting person to know. Well, I expect the owner will turn up one of these days. You might mention among your men friends that my niece has found an expensive-looking suede jacket in her hall closet. Somebody from the neighborhood may have left it here and forgotten where it is. Beth told us Mr. Cox used to entertain quite a lot."

"I wouldn't know. Cox never bothered much about Pam and me. Well, thanks for the coffee and the hot tip. I sure am grateful to get that inside dope on the Con Fed split."

"He ought to be," Harriet remarked after Jenny had closed the door on their uninvited guest. "I've put a tidy piece of change in that young man's pocket, if he doesn't louse up the deal. And now I think this old gal's had enough excitement for one day. If you'll excuse me, I'm going to hit the sack."

8

Morning brought Beth Firbelle and an armload of chrysanthemums. "Aunt Marguerite thought you might as well enjoy these before the frost gets them. It was down around freezing last night."

"How lovely!" Jenny helped her untangle the stems from the cord of the ever-present crocheted drawstring bag. "Won't you come in for a cup of coffee? Aunt Harriet and I are still trying to wake each other up."

"Thanks, but I don't dare take the time. We're getting ready for our annual rummage sale at the church, and Aunt Marguerite promised I'd help. I ought to have been down there half an hour ago. You wouldn't have any white elephants you'd care to donate, I don't suppose?"

"Haven't I just! This place is full of them. Was Mr. Cox's taste really all this rotten, or did he just inherit the furniture from whoever was here before him, the way I did?"

"I don't think Mr. Cox did much about the furnishings. Most of the stuff was already here. Old Mrs. Brady—you wouldn't know about her, of course, but she lived here for a while after she broke up her big place, where Greg and Pam are living now. Anyway, she brought a lot of things with her when she came. The furniture was terribly out of scale for this little house, but it was what she'd been used to and I suppose she couldn't bear to part with it."

"I can," said Jenny. "If you want to send somebody around with a truck, I'll be glad to fill it up. I'm sick of tripping over fake oriental tabourets and those ghastly jardinieres that look as if they'd been glazed with melted peanut butter and then left to mildew. Don't you think I ought to clean this place right out and start fresh, Aunt Harriet?"

"It's the only thing to do."

The older woman had come to the door in her brand-new blue lounging robe, cradling a mug of hot coffee in competent, heavily veined hands. "Good morning, Beth. Aren't you kind to bring us all those flowers. And did I hear you say rummage sale?"

"Yes, it's Saturday from ten till six. Would you like to come?"

"Why not? I don't think I've been to one in forty years. Is there something Jenny and I can do to help?"

"Well, if you're really serious about contributing all these wonderful things?"

"We really are," Jenny assured her. "Can you send

somebody over with a wagon or whatever, or shall I try to squeeze them into that bug of mine? I'll have to make about seventeen trips if I bring the stuff myself."

"I can arrange for a pickup."

Beth made her farewells and bustled off, the drawstring bag swinging purposefully. Harriet Compton put on a washable shirtwaist she'd bought at Louise's Boutique, tied one of Jenny's blouses around her waist by the sleeves to serve as an apron, and started lugging.

"We might as well pile everything beside the driveway," she panted, staggering out with a truly dreadful jardiniere, complete with a bouquet of dusty peacock feathers. "Why anybody would deliberately choose to live with a thing like this is beyond me. My mother wouldn't even allow peacock feathers in the house. She claimed they were bad luck."

"Too bad my father didn't know that," said Jenny.

"Jenny, I'm sorry! I didn't mean to—"

"That's all right, Aunt Harriet. A person can't feel much grief for somebody she's never known."

She fiddled with one of the bedraggled plumes. "I don't know what I feel, to tell you the truth. I was brought up to believe my father was the worst creature that ever crawled the face of the earth, but as they say, there are two sides to every story. I hate to think I've been prejudiced by his leaving me all that money, but at least it shows he never forgot me, and he wanted to look after me in the end. That's something, isn't it?"

"Yes, Jenny, that's something. Come on, let's get the rest of this trash out of the house. Maybe it will change the luck."

Throwing away the clutter was a great catharsis. An hour later, Jenny's emotional state and the interior of the carriage house were both vastly improved.

"I can't believe it!" she exclaimed. "You can actually walk through the living room without barking your shins on anything. I wish I had the nerve to chuck that crummy old overstuffed parlor suite, too."

Miss Compton laughed. "Don't get carried away. We do need something to sit on, you know."

"Yes, but does it have to be something like that? I'd like a pretty little settee and maybe one of those Shaker rocking chairs. This room could be so pleasant with the right furniture."

"Yes, it could," Harriet Compton agreed. "The proportions are good, and that fireplace with the cherrywood mantel is absolutely perfect, now that we can get a decent look at it. You could turn this old carriage house into a real showplace, if you decide to stay here."

"Why shouldn't I stay? It's my house, isn't it?"

All of a sudden, Jenny felt a ferocious pride of ownership. "This is the only real home I've ever had, where I can do exactly as I please without my mother's relatives standing over me finding fault. I'll stay as long as I want," she finished childishly.

"I was only wondering how long you'd want to," drawled Harriet Compton.

Jenny flushed. "I'm sorry. That was pretty silly of me. Of course, I shan't want to roost here for the rest of my life. Once I've done what I came for, maybe I'll take a wad of my father's money, if there's any left to take, and go see the world. But it would be sort of cozy to know this little house was waiting for me when I got tired of traveling and wanted to come home."

"It would, wouldn't it? I hope you can, Jenny."

"Oh well, perhaps I wouldn't like it so much after all. Living in the house where my father was murdered—" She slammed her fist into a red and yellow sofa cushion. "I'd like to take that suede jacket and shove it into the rummage sale!"

"Go ahead, if that's the way you feel about it," said Harriet Compton.

"And destroy the one real clue we've got? You don't think I meant it, do you? I'm just blowing off steam. Besides, we've let Greg Bauer know we have the jacket. Maybe he'll spread the word, and somebody will come looking for it. Or come looking for you. It's going to be a jolt when whoever mailed it finds out it's landed right back here on Packard Street."

"You can say that again," Harriet agreed. "I think we can cross Greg Bauer off the list as far as the jacket's concerned, though, don't you? I'd be willing to swear he'd never seen it before."

"He was just sorry it didn't fit." Jenny snorted. "Tough luck on Sue Giles if Greg turns out to be innocent after all. Come to think of it, I'll bet Sue's own husband's about the right size. I wish we'd thought of the jacket while she was here. We could have said we came across it while we were cleaning the junk out and wondered if Bill might have left it sometime when he was visiting Mr. Cox."

Harriet shook her now slightly disheveled head. "No good. Don't you recall how bitter Sue was about their never getting invited to Cox's parties? What occasion would Bill have to forget he'd left an expensive suede jacket here?"

"Plenty of occasions, maybe. As the next-door neighbor, he'd have a better chance than anybody else to sneak over here at night and—and do things without being caught."

"I'm not saying he didn't. I only meant that Sue didn't want us to think he could have. As to opportunity, the Gileses both had every chance in the world. They might have been up to something together. More probably, they could have seen somebody around here the night Cox was killed and didn't say anything for fear of getting involved. Lots of people are like that, you know. Or maybe they knew the murderer as a friend or a relative."

"Which could mean anyone in Meldrum, judging from what I learned at that party they gave," said Jenny. "They could even have helped the killer to get rid of the jacket. I'll bet they wouldn't have had any trouble getting that piece of wrapping paper out of this house to mail the package in. Or they might have taken in a package ages ago for that old woman who used to live here and wound up keeping the wrapper for some reason or other."

"They may even have a key to this house," Harriet agreed. "People do often leave door keys with their closest neighbors. And you told me yourself that Sue's frightened about something. Furthermore, we both saw how quick she was to steer us away from thinking she and her husband were friendly with James. Then she tossed us that earful about James and the Firbelles. Makes you wonder, doesn't it?"

"But how could they have gotten your address to send

you the jacket? You've never met either of them before, surely?"

"Jenny, how am I supposed to answer that? To begin with, I haven't so much as caught sight of Bill Giles yet. He may be my long-lost cousin, for all I know. As for Sue, I don't recall ever meeting her, but that doesn't mean I haven't. Accountants don't handle their clients' day-to-day bookkeeping, you know. We just go in and spend a day or two at the end of a fiscal year or at income tax time when the books have to be gone over. Some companies employ literally hundreds of clerical workers, and they all tend to look alike when you've seen as many of them as I have. Sue could have worked in some office I visited and remembered me because having the accountant in always puts the boss in a tizzy."

"I can imagine," said Jenny. "Uncle Fred always comes unglued when he's having his taxes done. I suppose you might make an impression on the staff simply because you didn't come often."

"Yes, and maybe not a favorable one."

"Especially if they were cooking the books, as you say. Maybe you sent Bill Giles to jail for embezzling, and now they're out to get you!"

Harriet only shrugged. "Stranger things have happened, my dear. Sue's got a mean streak in her wide enough to think of revenge, I'd say, judging from the way she was ripping her neighbors up the back yesterday. And if she's scared, she must have some reason to be. Though that could be just nerves because she's living next door to the house where James was killed. In any case, I'd say we ought to check out the Gileses pretty thoroughly, wouldn't you?"

"Let's invite them to one of those intimate little dinners my father never asked them to. How about Sunday night?"

"Let's see how things work out. We don't want the invitation to look too contrived. Maybe we could have them over for dessert and coffee some night during the week, after we've got the place fixed up a bit. New curtains or whatever would make a reasonable excuse. I notice Sue's taking a keen interest in our junk pile, even though she's trying not to let us see her peeking around the curtain over there."

"I expect everybody on the street is doing the same," said Jenny. "Too bad my Aunt Martha isn't here to catch the show. She spends half her time spying on the neighbors. I wonder if anybody saw Greg Bauer sneaking around the place last night. He must be pretty desperate to come hunting stock market tips from me."

"Maybe that wasn't all he thought he'd get," drawled Harriet Compton. "Visiting lonely ladies is probably his favorite pastime. I'll bet this was the first time he's done it to have his palm read, though."

"I still can't believe he was serious about that Peruvian stock; but he certainly acted as if he was, don't you think, Aunt Harriet?"

"I'm just glad I'm not handling the accounts at the place where he works, wherever that may be," the older woman agreed. "He may already have taken a dip into the boss's cash. Probably gambled and got in over his head. That type always does. Bauer is the classic small-time embezzler: greedy, vain, and stupid enough to think he can get away with it. For his family's sake, I hope I threw a scare into him before it's too late. He can bail himself out if he doesn't botch that Con Fed deal."

"Then he'll be hounding you for another hot tip."

"Let him. Maybe I'll set up in Meldrum as an investment broker. I couldn't do any worse than some of the so-called experts. As an old friend of mine used to say, 'if they're all so smart, how come they're not all millionaires themselves?' "

A sad little smile curved Harriet Compton's lips, then she shook her head, as if to rid her mind of something she'd rather not think about. "Well, Jenny, can you think of anything else to throw out?"

"That had better be it for now. I do hope Beth's found somebody to cart this junk away. I also hope we don't have to chase over to the rummage sale and buy any of it back. I'm sure I've gotten rid of at least six things we're going to need later, like that gruesome lamp with the icky green shade that was on the dining room table."

"How desperate would you have to be to need that thing back? If that's what James used to light up those cozy little dinner parties of his, I should think the guests would all have come down with indigestion."

Jenny laughed. "I love the way you keep calling him James, as if he were some black sheep relative of yours."

"I didn't realize I was doing that." Harriet Compton actually blushed, as if she'd been caught doing something improper. "Maybe it's on account of those slipcovers. He must have been quite a person, if he had the guts to buy something that wild."

"Maybe you knew him," said Jenny.

"But I—"

"I don't mean known, but met, the way you said you might have run across Sue Giles somewhere. I wish we had a picture of him."

"You didn't find any snapshots or anything around the house?"

"No. There were no personal papers of any kind. No clothes, either. Maybe the murderer took them." The black mood was back. "Maybe he was tied up with the Mafia or something. How do I know where he got all that money? Living here under an assumed name—"

"Lower your voice and come inside." Harriet Compton's voice lashed out low and sharp. "For God's sake, use your head. Don't go shouting it all over the neighborhood."

Appalled at her loss of control, Jenny turned to follow Harriet Compton into the carriage house. They hadn't quite reached the door when a large, sleek station wagon pulled into the overgrown driveway.

What ghastly luck! Just as she'd gotten to the point where she needed to get it all off her chest, the rummage sale messenger had to arrive. And naturally the driver had to be Lawrence MacRae.

His companion was a white-haired, crimson-faced woman in bristly wool tweeds and a lurid tam o'shanter. This must be the grandmother with the tartan cat. She was out and tugging at a spindle-legged tabouret almost before the car stopped beside the junk pile.

"Pr-r-riceless! The gr-randest heap o' trash we've had in thir-rty year-rs!"

Her r's rolled out like the snare drums of the Queen's

Own Highlanders. She hurled the tabouret into the back of her grandson's lavishly equipped station wagon, then wheeled to stick out a small, square hand at Harriet who, with Jenny, had, of course, gone back to help with the loading.

"How d'ye do? I'm Elspeth Gillespie."

Harriet Compton managed to return the determined handshake without wincing. "How do you do? I'm Harriet Compton. My grandmother was a Gillespie. And this is my niece, Jenny Plummer."

"Oh, aye? That one's gr-randmother was nae Gillespie, I'll be bound."

The Scotswoman's fierce blue eyes raked over Jenny's ivory-cream complexion and eyebrows so jetty they gleamed in the sun like a black cat's fur. "She has the look of a tinker lassie tae me."

"Cross my palm with silver and I'll tell your fortune, pretty lady," Jenny whined pertly. Maybe she did have gipsy blood in her. That could explain a lot of things.

"I hear-rd aboot your fortune-tellin'."

The ruddy face remained grave, but there was a twinkle in the bluebell eyes now. "Callin' doon black doom on the head o' her-r leddyship over yon. Weel, ye won't be the fair-rst, Jenny lass, nor maybe the last. She's a tough auld hen for a' her air-rs an' gr-races. Lawrence, ye mannerless lout, are ye no' goin' to mek your-r manners an' lend a hand?"

The tall young man with the absurd red mustache slid out from behind the wheel, where he'd been silently enjoying his grandmother's performance, and came around to be introduced to Miss Compton.

"Did ye ever-r see twa reelatives who looked less

alike?" Mrs. Gillespie demanded. "Weel, speak up, lad. Ye can mak' enough clishmaclaver when ye're o' mind to."

"I'm trying to think of something I can say without getting my face slapped," MacRae answered, giving Jenny a straight look.

Harriet Compton came to the rescue. "Jenny takes after me in nothing but her temperament. That's why we have to hang together. The rest of the family can't stand either one of us." She slung an arm around Jenny and gave her shoulders a friendly, warning squeeze.

"Oh, so ye've family, tinker-r lassie? I'd got the notion ye were a lone or-rphan."

"Far from it." Here was a sterling opportunity for Jenny to tell the truth. "My father is dead, but my mother and my uncles and aunts and cousins are alive in droves. That's the reason I got away from them all and came here to Meldrum. I'm trying to write a book," she explained, with the proper modest laugh at her own pretensions.

"Aye."

Mrs. Gillespie gave her a satisfied nod and went back to stuffing odds and ends into the station wagon.

"That's it, Gran," Lawrence MacRae said after a while. "I'll have to come back for another load. Or two, or three." The pile didn't seem to have diminished at all.

"I'd help, but my car won't hold much," Jenny apologized. "When I bought it, I didn't realize how much fetching and carrying is involved with country life."

"You don't call this country living, do you?" MacRae sounded as if he thought that was pretty funny.

"It's the closest I've come to it," Jenny retorted.

"Well, cheer up, tinker lassie. You'll probably be hitching up the old caravan again pretty soon."

9

Lawrence MacRae backed out of the driveway, leaving Jenny to sputter among the peacock feathers.

"Did you hear that, Aunt Harriet? What's he trying to do, run me out of town?"

"Good question. That's the chap you had the little set-to with out in the back yard after Sue Giles's party, as I recall. I think we'd better engineer a private session with young MacRae, too."

"How can we? He doesn't even like me."

"So what? He's part Gillespie, isn't he? I'll hold a gathering of the clan. That can't do any harm, can it?"

"How am I supposed to know?"

Harriet Compton shrugged. "You sure do know how to liven up a party, Jenny. All right, we don't know; but what are we supposed to do, sit on our hands and wait? If we keep stirring the pot, something's bound to bubble to the surface sooner or later. Sure, it's a risk, but that's what life is about, in case you haven't found out yet. Now what was it you were going to tell me about your father?"

Jenny took a deep breath. "His name wasn't James Cox. It was Jason Cirak."

"The producer who made *The Refugees?* That was a wonderful movie, Jenny. It still is."

"Is it really? My mother would never let me see it. Anyway, after that he made a few that weren't so good, I guess, and then he never did anything else, so far as the family could ever find out. So where did he get over half a million dollars to leave to me?"

"Movie producers make a lot of money, Jenny."

"Sure, while they're producing. And from what I can gather, he blew every nickel as fast as it came in. Father thought he was the Great Gatsby."

Jenny's voice quivered. So the hurt hadn't gone away, after all. "I'm only speaking from hearsay. I can't remember my father at all. He walked out on us when I was still a baby. I didn't even know he was dead until I got a letter asking me to contact his lawyers. When they told me about the money, I thought it must be some kind of crazy joke. Uncle Fred and the rest didn't think it was funny at all. They assumed he'd robbed a bank."

"I gather they weren't exactly fans of Jason Cirak."

"They took a dim view of the way he dumped his wife and kid back on the family to support."

"Was that a hardship for your uncle and the rest? Are you wondering if you ought to turn your money over to them by way of recompense?"

"Not for one second, thank you! Don't think they haven't been bending my ear about that. Naturally they're all ripping because father left it to me instead of his lawfully wedded wife."

"There was never a divorce, right?"

"Not to my knowledge. I believe my father did write to my mother a few times, begging her to divorce him because he wasn't coming back. He'd found another woman he wanted to marry, and he was dumb enough to say so. That was the main reason she wouldn't. Mama was always the spoiled baby of the family. I think she realized she'd never want to get married again herself, so it suited her better to play dog in the manger. In some ways I don't blame him for ditching her. I just wish he'd taken me, too."

Jenny gulped. "Anyway, I'm not going to give the Plummers one red cent. Grandfather Plummer left his estate for the whole family to share, so Mama was as entitled as the rest, if it came to that. Uncle Fred's only the administrator, and he's had more fun doling out the money a penny at a time and telling me how grateful I ought to be for a roof over my head than he'd have gotten any other way. I don't see where I owe him anything. I did think of sending some to my mother, but she'd only hand it over to Uncle Fred, or stick it in the bank so she could leave it to me when she dies. What's the sense in that?"

"None whatsoever," said Harriet Compton. "Do what feels right to you. Sounds as if they managed to make life pretty grim for you."

"Well, I'll tell you one thing. I'm never going to insist

on doing my duty by anybody and make them hate me for it."

"I should hope not. So you didn't think it was your duty to come here to Meldrum to try to clear your father's name? You're just doing it for kicks, right?"

"You had to say that, didn't you? I couldn't stand listening to the digs and the endless questions about how a man who never did an honest day's work in his life happened to wind up with all that money."

"It's not true that Jason Cirak never did an honest day's work in his life," snapped Harriet Compton. "He slaved his guts out to support himself after he landed in this country without family or friends and hardly a penny in his pocket. And he produced a film that's a classic. Whatever else he may have done, you've got to hand him that."

Jenny gave her a doubtful smile. "I'm not used to hearing anybody say a good word for my father."

"Never lose sight of the facts, Jenny, no matter what anybody tries to tell you. The eagle's a predator and a scavenger and a slob around his nest, but he's still the most magnificent bird that flies. A man who has to claw his way from the bottom to the top may stamp on a few faces as he passes them on the ladder. I don't say it's respectable or decent, but I do say you might as well not expect an eagle to turn into a barnyard rooster because it's never going to happen. You'll know that by the time you're an old woman like me."

"Don't talk about being old. You can't be old yet. I've only just found you." Jenny stopped, surprised at herself.

"How can you matter so much when I don't even know for sure if you're with me or against me?"

"But you're willing to take me on faith for the time being?" Harriet Compton seemed to have something wrong with her eye, for she suddenly began dabbing at it with her handkerchief. "Thanks, Jenny. Oh, oh. Here comes Flash Gordon again. He didn't lose any time at the church, did he? Why don't you go tackle him alone this time?"

"If you say so." Jenny headed outside to the junk pile again as MacRae pulled into the yard. She was off to a bad start even before she got to him. He climbed out of the car with a camera in his hand.

"Get back by the door, will you? I want to get a shot of you coming out of the house."

"What for?" she demanded.

"Publicity for the local papers. Meldrum Woman Gives Her All for Church Rummage Sale. Real dynamic human interest stuff. Turn toward me."

"No!"

Jenny wasn't having her picture in any paper. Publicity about Jason Cirak's daughter, now living in the house where her father was almost certainly murdered, would be the last thing she needed. How did she know who might see it? For all she knew, somebody she'd gone to school with might be living in the area now, or some former neighbor of the Plummers. They'd come charging over here wanting to know why Jenny Cirak had changed her name, or worse still, asking the neighbors. She threw an arm across her face.

"Don't you dare!"

"Why not, for Pete's sake? Where's your civic pride?"

"Never mind my civic pride. I haven't lived here long enough to have any. Furthermore"—she'd better come up with a plausible excuse—"I'm a disaster. These clothes—"

"Marks of honest toil in a worthy cause. Hold still a second." He was squinting through his view-finder. "This won't hurt a bit."

That was what he thought.

"Wait, I have a better idea." Hiding her face, Jenny dashed to the junk pile and picked up the biggest and most loathesome jardiniere. "Why don't I be lugging this monstrosity? That should make a fun picture."

"Okay, if you insist. Turn this way a little and take a step forward. Fine, hold it. Now lower that spittoon thing a little. The feather duster stuff is hiding your face."

As if she didn't know. Instead of lowering it, Jenny hitched the pot a few inches higher. "Don't you think I look more glamorous peeking through the peacock feathers? Hurry, can't you? This thing weighs a ton."

MacRae shrugged and snapped. "How come you're so camera-shy, tinker lassie?"

"I've been stealing chickens, of course. Isn't that what we gipsy rovers do for kicks? I wouldn't know about roving photographers. Here, this is for you."

She shoved the jardiniere into his arms. "Could we move it, please? I was hoping to get this mess cleaned up as quickly as possible."

"I'll bet you were." He gave her an enigmatic look across the peacock feathers. "You fascinate me, tinker lassie."

"How kind of you to say so. It's the psychic vibrations,

98

I suppose. Are you quite sure you don't want to have your palm read?"

"I'm giving the matter some careful thought."

"Really? It's so nice to know you're able to think."

Jenny began slamming her father's castoffs into the station wagon as fast as her arms would move. Her own single thought was to get Lawrence MacRae and his dangerous camera out of her yard.

10 ❦❦❦

"MacRae scares me, Aunt Harriet. I think he knows something."

The older woman nodded matter-of-factly. "That wouldn't surprise me a bit. That's why we've got to talk to him one way or another, Jenny."

"I'm afraid I've picked the wrong way. He was going to take my picture just now, for publicity about the sale, or so he said. I didn't dare let him, so I got nasty."

"Yes, I saw that touching little tableau out there. Why don't you change into something a shade more presentable, and we'll pop over to see what's happening at the rummage sale?"

"Why can't I go as I am? We can say we've come to help."

"Not me, young woman. I've done my bit, and we don't

want to get stuck there too long anyway. Besides, your boyfriend might decide to take another picture of you helping, and what if there weren't any more peacock feathers around? Go on, take a quick shower while I make a bit of lunch, and let's go over there."

"I'd like to know whether he was really doing it for publicity or just trying to get my goat."

"Both, maybe. If we get down there in time, we might be able to find out."

"All right, I can take a hint when somebody hits me over the head with it."

Jenny rinsed off the grime and got dressed in a bright kingfisher blue sweater and skirt Harriet Compton had insisted on her buying at Louise's. It was infinitely superior to anything she'd dared pick out for herself so far.

"I just hope the Cirak fortune hasn't turned back to mice and pumpkins by the time I get the bills for all this stuff I've been splurging on," she remarked as they ate a quick sandwich.

"Think positive," said Harriet Compton. "That color becomes you, but do me a favor and donate the wig to the rummage sale."

"You don't think it's a good disguise?"

"What I think wouldn't bear repeating so near a church. Tie a scarf over your head or something if you must. Or borrow MacRae's mustache. Come on, let's move. Do you know where this place is?"

"I think so. We can walk it in about three minutes, unless you're too tired."

"I'm too tired. Let's take the car, just in case it turns out you thought wrong."

But they didn't have any trouble finding the church. MacRae's station wagon stood in the yard along with some other cars, and the bouquet of peacock feathers was still sitting beside the door. They went up the walk and in the door, carrying the leftover bits and pieces they'd brought along as an excuse for barging in.

The church hall had the unmistakable odor of poverty and sanctity Jenny had known since her Sunday school days. Too few members of a congregation that had once overflowed the barny American Gothic building every Sunday morning were now struggling to keep the old-time religion alive in a world that hadn't time to bother with it anymore. The usual dedicated handful were milling around the big, cold basement room, trying to relieve its dingy bleakness with the usual sparse, amateurish decorations, setting up the usual long, rickety tables, covering them with rolls of white wrapping paper scrounged from somewhere, heaping them with the donated junk that had become the lifeblood of the Church Militant.

Beth Firbelle was in the vanguard, her baggy puce pullover and skirt more or less protected by a grimy kitchen apron. She was so busy bossing the show she didn't so much as glance around when her new acquaintances walked in.

"We've got to get all the big stuff over by the piano," she was ordering. "Larry, take one end of this daybed. No, don't you try to lift it, Mr. Morton. You'll hurt your back again. Come on, Jack, lend a hand."

Her cousin obediently took hold of the heavy, outmoded sofa bed and helped MacRae move it the entire length of the room. Jenny heard Harriet Compton draw in her breath, but when she glanced over, the older woman's face was a noncommittal blank.

Of course, they didn't remain unnoticed for long. Elspeth Gillespie spotted them first.

"Come in, leddies! Mak' yoursel's to hame."

"We only came to drop these off." Harriet Compton picked her way down a cluttered aisle, holding out her last few offerings. "Is there anything we can do?"

"You've done wonders already." That was Beth Firbelle, bustling up to them, wiping her dusty hands on her filthy apron. "We can't tell you how grateful we are for all those wonderful things you sent."

"You'd have gotten more if Aunt Harriet hadn't followed me around reminding me we need something to eat with and sleep on tonight," said Jenny. "I'd have made a clean sweep. I've decided to redo the whole place."

"How wonderful to have a home of one's own, where you can do exactly as you please." Beth spoke barely above a whisper, so that Elspeth Gillespie, standing a stiff ten paces away, wouldn't overhear, but the longing in her voice came through with bitter clarity.

"Beth, where do we put these dishes?" Jack Firbelle's querulous inquiry called her back to the business at hand.

"I've already told you twice," she snapped back. "All the china goes on that big table by the door. Honestly, if they appoint me committee chairman one more time. . . ."

Beth darted away, her rump-sprung skirt bagging out behind her.

"Aye, an' if they don't, they'll hear-r about it," snorted

Elspeth Gillespie. "She's a wor-rker, I'll hand her-r that. Wad ye care to see upstair-rs, Miss Compton?"

"I'd be honored."

As Harriet accepted the invitation in a proper spirit of reverent curiosity, Jenny could see the thought going through Elspeth Gillespie's head: a decent, respectable body. Well, she was, even though Jenny had a hunch Harriet's notions of decency might be somewhat different from old Elspeth's. Now, where was that grandson of hers? Jenny knew she'd better keep an eye on him to make sure he didn't snap any more pictures. Ah, there he was, toiling among the bric-a-brac. She went over to the table.

"Where's your camera, Mr. MacRae? I'd be glad to take a picture of you to demonstrate your civic pride."

"You're a funny lady," he snarled. "Here, take this. You never know when you may want it."

He plucked a crumpled halloween mask out from among the debris and thrust it across the table at her.

"You're funny, too, Mr. MacRae."

Jenny made rather a thing of turning her back on him and the mask and walked over to where Beth was now hanging other people's old clothes on a rack made of rusty water pipes.

"What lovely things!" she exclaimed to Jenny. "Look, can you imagine anyone's giving away a dress as pretty as this? I wouldn't mind buying it myself."

Jenny couldn't see anything special about the garment Beth was holding out for her to look at, except that it was a definite improvement over the clumsily home-cobbled outfit Beth had on; but she agreed out of politeness. "Yes, it is nice. Why don't you take it?"

"Oh, I couldn't do that."

Marguerite Firbelle's niece gave her a sad little smile and hung the dress on the rack. Jenny stuck one or two things on wire coat hangers for her, then drifted away. She sensed that Beth didn't much want her help, and she'd worn too many of her cousins' hand-me-downs in her own less affluent days to find the job anything but depressing.

Poor Beth! Of course it wouldn't do for a Firbelle to go parading around Meldrum in something she'd bought at a rummage sale; but what a rotten shame her aunt didn't break down and buy her something fit to wear. Mrs. Firbelle certainly did all right by her beloved son. Even with an armload of cracked saucers, Jack looked like an advertisement for the well-dressed man. One could easily get to hate a woman like Marguerite Firbelle.

11

Miss Compton and Mrs. Gillespie were returning from their inspection of the sanctuary. Jenny could hear the r's bouncing off the walls as they came downstairs.

"An' so I r-reminded the meenister-r last Thur-rsday."

Lawrence MacRae went over to meet his grandmother. "What do you say, Gran? Done enough good works for one day? I'm ready to gang alang hame and put on the feedbag."

"Aye, when were ye ever-r not? Miss Compton, will ye no' come an' sup a dish o' tea wi' us?"

"Why, thank you, that sounds delightful. Unless my niece has something else planned?"

"Br-ring the tinker-r lassie wi' ye. She's welcome as the flower-rs in May."

Mrs. Gillespie's face beamed like a fierce red sun under its aureole of flying white hair. Jenny didn't much relish the idea of sharing her dish of tea with Lawrence MacRae, but how could one turn down this Caledonian version of Mrs. Santa Claus?

Anyway, the house was worth going to see. Old Elspeth's living room was as ferociously merry as the woman herself. Everything, from the sofa to the tea cozy, was upholstered in one of several clan tartans, each of whose significance she explained in a spate of consonants. The bagpipes and sporran of her husband, the late Colin Gillespie, hung in a place of honor over the fireplace. Above them was an ebulliently horrible portrait in oils of the patriarch himself, wearing the sporran and playing the pipes with his plaid, his kilt, and his bush of red whiskers all flapping in the gale he must have been generating through his chanter.

"That portrait is what made me decide to be a photographer instead of a painter," the grandson told the guests with an irreverent grin.

He seemed less hostile here in his grandmother's house. Jenny had to wonder if he was basically a friendly chap with a chip on his shoulder about something. Since there'd hardly been time for him to work up a really good grudge against herself, much less Harriet Compton, could that something relate in any way to her father's presence in Meldrum and his sudden mysterious death? But why pick on her? For all MacRae knew, Jenny had never even met James Cox.

Whatever Lawrence's problem might be, his grandmother didn't share it, that was plain. She was scolding him now, letting him know he needn't think he could get away with anything just because he was so obviously the apple of her eye.

"Do ye stop pokin' fun at your ain flesh an' bluid. Mek the leddies a bit o' fire to warm them while I set the pot tae draw."

Mrs. Gillsepie chugged off like the Little Engine That Could and came steaming back in no time at all behind a tea wagon laden with hot scones, hot crumpets, short-bread, oatcake, Dundee cake, Scotch bun, Scotch marma-lade, and bone china teacups bearing the crest of Clan MacRae. She got her party comfortably sorted out around the fire, poured out their tea, loaded their plates with goodies, then settled down to a comfortable pumping session.

"Ye say your grandmother-r was a Gillespie, Miss Compton?"

It took three cups of tea and a great deal of oatcake to determine exactly which branch of the family tree Aunt Harriet's forbears had perched on. At last Mrs. Gillespie satisfied herself that Harriet would have been the late Colin's seventh cousin once removed and thus entitled to full rights and privileges as a member of his family.

According to the mythical connection between herself and Jenny's parents that Harriet Compton was then obliged to weave, that made Jenny and Lawrence eighth cousins, also once removed. One removal from Lawrence MacRae would do her nicely, Jenny decided, and she only wished it could be a permanent one. Why didn't he go roving off and photograph something far, far away instead of sitting over there beside the tea cart, glowering at her from under those bushy red eyebrows? What had she done to make him look like that?

Under the circumstances she couldn't manage much in the way of light conversation. He wasn't talking either, but the two older women made sure there were no awkward gaps in the conversation. They'd progressed from genealogy to neighbors by now. Mrs. Gillespie naturally understood the concern of a respectable, God-fearing maiden aunt like Seventh Cousin Harriet as to what sort of neighborhood her literary-minded young niece had moved into. She dissected every household in the general vicinity with the expertise and precision of a brain surgeon.

Most of the residents, it appeared, were decent enough folk in their ain ways. On the subject of the Firbelles, however, Elspeth was coldly polite and none too forthcoming. Beth was conceded to be a great church worker, not that she had much chance to be anything else, puir body. Marguerite was a woman of elegance, not that elegance was quite the thing in a place like Meldrum. Elspeth smoothed down the lap of her own sensible tweed skirt, adjusted the collar of her sensible plaid blouse, and passed the scones again.

"Well, I suppose one couldn't expect such an attractive woman to wear widows' weeds forever," Miss Compton remarked as she helped herself to more marmalade. "I understand she had a near miss from being widowed a second time."

"Oh?" The Scotswoman's white eyebrows shot up behind her cloud of hair. "Is that a fact?"

"As to whether it's a fact or not, I'm not in a position

to say." The accountant buttered a scone with elaborate care. "In any event, it's common talk around town, or so I gather. Jenny's next-door neighbor told us Mrs. Firbelle had been all set to marry James Cox, that man who had the carriage house before Jenny and got himself killed, nobody seems to know how."

"Aye, that was a deep meestery," snapped Elspeth Gillespie. "An' a bigger-r meestery to me is where Sue Giles got her-r information. No' but what she keeps that lang nose o' her-rs glued to the windowpane from mor-rn till night. How that bur-rglar ever got awa' wi'oot her bein' there to spy him an' cry mur-rder is another thing I'll never understand. Puir James Cox would for once hae been the better-r for her snoopin'. Ah weel, the Lord giveth an' the Lord taketh awa' accordin' to His ain time an' pleasure. Though whiles, as the old woman of Edinburgh said, I think he might be guidit. There's them that could hae better been spared than James Cox."

"Then you knew him personally?"

"Aye, that I did."

"And you don't really believe he intended to marry Mrs. Firbelle."

"That," said Mrs. Gillespie, plunging her serving knife savagely into the heart of the fruit-filled Scotch bun, "I can positeevely assur-re ye he did not."

"Indeed?" Harriet Compton packed a world of polite innuendo into those two syllables.

"I hae my reasons."

Mrs. Gillespie was saying a lot more than mere words, too. Was it only the flickering of the firelight, or was that a coy expression on the woman's by-no-means-unattractive face? Elspeth must have been a bonny lassie indeed when Colin Gillespie first piped his way into her heart. Had James Cox been playing a similar tune?

"I'm sorry," said Miss Compton. "I hope I haven't said anything to distress you. I had no idea you were a close personal friend of Mr. Cox. Jenny and I have been wondering about him, naturally, but we didn't mean to—"

"Ah weel, there's many a woman has given her-rself notions about James Cox, I'll be bound. Mebbe you'd like tae see what a fine figur-re of a man he was? Lawrence, show the leddies those peectur-res you took."

MacRae, who had barely opened his mouth for the past half-hour except to put food in it, set down his tartan tea-cup and unfolded himself from his tartan armchair. He left the room and came back with a glossy black-and-white print in his hand.

"This one's the best. I took it only a few days before he was killed. Cox made an interesting subject."

MacRae was an artist with his lens, no doubt about that, and Jason Cirak was a photographer's dream of the perfect model. He'd had a magnificent head of gray hair, deep-set eyes that must have been as close to black as Jenny's were, a strongly defined nose, and lips that showed a warm, humorous curve over a neatly trimmed imperial. The beard came somehow as a surprise to the daughter who'd been so sure she didn't remember him at all.

"I didn't know he had a beard."

It was a stupid thing to say, but it was the only thing Jenny could think of as she stared down at her father's face. MacRae had caught him in profile, boldly jutting against a background of ice-covered branches, wearing the plaid jacket Greg Bauer had mentioned. His head was bare, his frost-colored mane tossed by the wind. Harriet was right. Her father had been an eagle.

How could she know this face so well? If she'd met this man on a street in Bangkok, she'd have gone up to him without a second's hesitation. What made her so sure?

"You don't care for the beard, tinker lassie?" MacRae was still beside her, watching her pore over the photograph. "Shall I take it off?"

"No. Don't spoil it."

Jenny tried to snatch the picture out of his reach, but MacRae got hold of it and made quick strokes with a retouching crayon.

"Don't worry, I have the negative. There, now how do you like it, Miss Plummer? Or should I say Miss Cox?"

Jenny knew now. The features were more rugged, yet the face was her own, in some subtle way she couldn't have explained but would never fail to recognize.

"I hope you didn't do that to be cruel, Larry." That was Harriet Compton, backing her up against this puzzling enemy. "Jenny didn't know how strangely like her father she is, even though she has her mother's delicate features. Her parents were separated when she was a baby, with great bitterness on the mother's side. I daresay this is the first photograph of James she's ever had a chance to see. Right, Jenny?"

"Yes," Jenny choked. "Mother never told me."

MacRae started to say something, perhaps to apologize, but Harriet's cool voice overrode his. "As you must know by now, Jenny inherited her father's property along with many of his characteristics. That's how she happens to be here in Meldrum. She'd been wanting a place of her own, and it seemed foolish to put this house on the market before she'd had a chance to decide whether she wanted to live here herself. Needless to say, she didn't really know anything about the circumstances of his death until after she got here, or she might have thought twice about coming. The estrangement was so complete that she didn't even know he was dead until she heard from his lawyers about settling the estate."

"But it was in the papers," Elspeth Gillespie protested.

"No doubt it was in the *Providence Journal* and the local weekly, but not in the out-of-town papers. At least if it was, none of the family ever saw it. Isn't that right, Jenny?"

"Yes. They were—they couldn't believe it. Uncle Fred—" Jenny had to give up trying to talk. Harriet, bless her, took over again.

"I believe it was Fred's idea that Jenny should use her mother's name instead of her father's. To avoid talk, you know. Naturally the neighbors would start wondering why James's daughter would be so quick to take over his property after he was dead, when she'd never once been to visit him while he was alive. Then the whole story would have had to come out, and Jenny'd have suffered a lot of needless embarrassment at a time when she had enough to cope with already. I'm sure you understand, Mrs. Gillespie."

MacRae wasn't quite ready to buy this explanation, Jenny could see, but his grandmother was nodding. "To be sur-re. Puir wee lassie!"

"I must admit Fred's always been stuffy about having

his sister's unfortunate marriage discussed in public," Harriet added.

Unnecessary lie number one. Fred and the rest discussed Jason Cirak often, with the same vindictive passion they still felt toward the late Franklin D. Roosevelt. They weren't the sort to waste a good grudge. Aunt Martha had been quite put out to learn that her sister-in-law's ill-chosen husband hadn't died in the gutter, as she had so often predicted he would.

Jenny wasn't about to contradict, however. Aunt Harriet's story was going down as easily as the scones and marmalade. Elspeth Gillespie's blue eyes welled with pity. Even Lawrence MacRae had begun to look ashamed of himself.

"Jenny hadn't the faintest notion there'd been anything out-of-the-way about James's death until Beth Firbelle told us yesterday morning and Sue Giles added a few more gory details later on. The lawyers had merely described it as an accident."

"But now, I don't know what to think," Jenny burst out. That, at any rate, was no lie. "I can't pretend to any terrible sense of loss over somebody I've never known; but all the same it's—I suppose it's been a shock," she finished lamely, looking into the fire and showing the profile so oddly reminiscent of Jason Cirak's.

"Aye, 'twould daunton the strongest amang us," Mrs. Gillespie soothed. "Lawrence, fetch the lass a wee sup o' my dandelion wine."

"I don't want any, thank you," said Jenny. "I'm all right. It was just the—the picture and everything."

"I'll be glad to make you a decent enlargement if you'd

care to have it." The photographer sounded thoroughly abashed, as well he might.

"Thank you, I'd love to have it. It's—like him, isn't it?"

"Verra like. James was a gr-and man." Elspeth Gillespie started gathering the tea things together. "It's queer tae think o' James havin' a young slip of a daughter. He must hae marrit late in life. Nae doot that's why he an' his wife didn't get alang. He needit a mair matur-re woman." Again there was that self-conscious little twitch of the lips.

"Yes, James was a good deal older than his wife in more ways than one," Aunt Harriet agreed placidly, just as though she knew all about Marion Plummer. "It's no wonder you didn't spot the likeness. Most people wouldn't. Your grandson, on the other hand, has a trained eye for faces. I suppose he noticed right away."

"It stuck out a mile, the minute I saw her at the Gileses'," said MacRae. "She even has some of her father's mannerisms: the way she holds her head, that hawklike stare she gives you when you've said something that doesn't hit her just right, the flying motions she makes with her hands when she's talking."

"Yes, I know. Sometimes when Jenny looks at me, it's almost as if I'm seeing James. It's enough to give you the shivers, when you think how long they'd been separated. I suppose it's either genes and chromosomes or Freud and infantile memories, depending on your point of view, though I must say I get rather fed up with that stuff, myself."

Harriet Compton picked up her gorgeous alligator bag and straightened her jacket. "Well, Jenny Maria, I think we ought to get along home and make sure we haven't thrown away any desperate necessities before it's too late to borrow them back. Thank you for the lovely tea, Mrs. Gillespie. It's been a great pleasure. You must come and see us when things are a bit less chaotic over at the carriage house."

Jenny said something, she didn't know what. She was too overwhelmed by the currents of feeling in that room to be capable of rational thought. There was her own shock on seeing her image caught in that dramatic photograph of her father. There was the grandson's contrition. There was old Elspeth's compassion and the flirtation she must have been carrying on with the alleged James Cox. And there was in Harriet Compton something most disconcerting of all: a tension driving this sensible, hardheaded, middle-aged businesswoman to get out of here before she burst all bounds of decorum and went into screaming hysterics.

12

"I move we skip dinner. After Cousin Elspeth's tea, a cup of bouillon would be about all I can manage."

Harriet Compton was doing her best to act like her normal self, although she wasn't making a very good job of it.

"I couldn't agree more," said Jenny. "What's the matter with you? You're about one step removed from a kitten fit."

"Have you ever thought of getting yourself burned as a witch? I'm supposed to be Old Stoneface."

The elderly accountant went over to the window and straightened a fold of the wild cretonne curtain that had been Jason Cirak's choice. "All right, I'll admit seeing your father's photograph gave me as big a jolt as it did you. It—I suppose it made the whole business real. Here was this vital, brilliant, unpredictable, wonderful man, living in this cut-up little house, sitting in these awful chairs, stumbling over all that junk we threw out today because he wouldn't think to get rid of it."

She left the curtain and came back to sit where Jason Cirak had no doubt sat on many an evening like this one. "And now he's gone. He simply isn't around any more. I don't know, Jenny. Young people can joke about dying, can even commit suicide because it's all a game and they think they'll snap out of it and go on tomorrow with whatever they didn't have time for today. Death isn't real then. But when you get to be our ages—I suppose James didn't mind so much, going as he did. It was better than sitting around getting old and sick and helpless. But still—"

It was a while before she managed to smile. "Okay, that's over. Shall I heat us some soup?"

"No," said Jenny. "Stay where you are. I'm going to light the fire and pour you a glass of sherry."

"Sterling idea. Warm the ancient bones and maybe I'll be able to act like a human being again."

"Oh, hush up, Aunt Harriet. Why should you be denied your share of feminine frailties just because you know how to do arithmetic?" Jenny slid a fat cushion behind Miss Compton's head, put a match to the ready-laid kindling, then went to get the sherry.

"Drink that and you'll feel better."

"Aren't you going to join me?"

"In a minute. I'll get the soup on."

Harriet Compton sat sipping her wine and gazing at

the flames. Jenny came back and did the same, until the soup boiled over and made a mess of the stove.

"I hope it isn't ruined," she remarked as she came back with two steaming mugs on a tray.

"The soup or the stove?" Harriet was beginning to sound like her usual self again.

"Either or both. Want some of these crackers?"

"Thanks. You're comfortable to be with, Jenny."

"You're the first person who's ever thought so."

"What do you want to bet I won't be the last?"

That didn't seem to call for any answer. Neither of them said any more until the soup was gone. After a while, Harriet Compton set her empty mug back on the tray.

"That hit the spot. Well, back to work. Let's balance the books. What have we got on the credit side so far?"

"Well, I suppose we can say we've established the fact that James Cox really was—my father. Jason Cirak. Do you think anybody could have recognized him as himself?"

"We're not thinking, we're adding up the facts. Okay, so there's one fact. What else?"

"I don't know whether it belongs on the credit or the debit side, but I'd say we've also learned my father was as big a wolf as my mother always claimed he was."

"Oh, you noticed, did you? Cousin Elspeth may have been indulging in a spot of wishful thinking, you know."

"She doesn't look like the imaginative type to me. Anyway, you just said yourself opinions don't count."

"Had to remember that, didn't you? So where does that put us? We've got Beth Firbelle hinting that James was after her aunt, Sue Giles virtually waltzing them down the aisle, and Elspeth Gillespie saying it's all hogwash because she herself was the fair-haired lady. However, not even Sue Giles seems to have gotten wind of the switch, and that I must say I find awfully hard to buy in as close-knit a neighborhood as this."

"I'm glad I'm not writing this story. Sounds like a pretty messy plot to me."

Jenny was being flippant to cover the hurt that was creeping back. Noble sport for an eagle, playing puss-in-the-corner with two elderly widows!

"So it does," Harriet Compton agreed, "and the sooner we straighten it out, the better. I'd like to know what Marguerite Firbelle herself thinks."

"You've got a fat chance of finding out."

"That's what you think, kid. I'll have the information by this time tomorrow night."

"What are you going to do, walk up and ask her?"

"I might just do that, if I can't think of anything more subtle." Harriet Compton wiggled her long, aristocratic feet out of her custom-made shoes and stretched out her toes toward the warmth.

After a pause, Jenny ventured. "Any more facts?"

"Sure. There's the fact that Jack Firbelle was heaving sofas around over there at the church.

"From which we deduce he's not such an invalid as his doting mama tries to tell people he is. I could have told you that."

"Ah," said the accountant, "but would I have believed you? It's one thing to call a man a phony because he goes around with a supercilious sneer on his face, but quite another job to prove he's cooking the books. If Jack really did have a heart condition, he'd have known better than to lift that heavy stuff, unless he's an abject masochist, which I seriously doubt. We also know Beth is quite aware of the fact that Jack's a healthy man or she wouldn't have asked him in the first place. Unless she absolutely hates his guts."

"For which I wouldn't blame her," said Jenny. "Honestly, the way he and his mother treat that poor woman makes me boil! Having to ask permission to leave the house for a little while, even. You can tell how desperately unhappy she is from the way she walks, the way she talks, and especially the way she dresses, in those droopy skirts and tops she tries to make for herself and doesn't know how. It's not that she doesn't care. She must care terribly, to put so much work into them even if they do look so awful when they're done. Honestly, if you'd seen her as I did, fingering the hand-me-downs at the rummage sale and wishing she dared buy herself something fit to wear, you'd have wanted to sit right down on the floor and bawl."

"Did she really do that?" Harriet Compton asked. "What puzzles me is why she sticks around Jack and his mother at all. Beth is a capable woman, even Elspeth Gillespie hands her that. She could get a job somewhere and support herself instead of having to do the poor relation bit."

"And deprive dear Aunt Marguerite of a free housemaid?" Jenny snorted. "The old biddy probably keeps stringing Beth along with the promise of a nice little inheritance if she toes the line. One of my mother's aunts has a widowed niece she's been pulling that line on for about thirty years. By the time the niece finally caught on, she was too old to make a change. That's what's happening to Beth, if you ask me. I'd like to take her aside and tell her a few things while there's still time for her to get out."

"If you'll take some advice from me, you'll keep your thoughts to yourself till you're sure Beth isn't doing just about what she wants to do," the older woman warned. "Families are strange, as you ought to have learned from your own experience. I don't think we're getting anywhere with this discussion, do you? What about a spot of innocent recreation till bedtime? I don't suppose you happen to play cribbage, by any chance? James must surely have left a board and a deck of cards around here somewhere."

"There's one in that desk we decided to keep. How did you know?"

"Good question. I haven't been rummaging through your private papers, if that's what you mean."

"Aunt Harriet, I never dreamed you were! It's just that I don't recall having opened the desk during the grand chuck-out. I went through it when I first came here. There wasn't much except some writing paper and a few receipted bills for fuel and whatnot. The cribbage board was in a separate little drawer with the cards, and I left it there. It gave me a—you know me and my feelings. And your mentioning it like that. . . ." Jenny's voice dwindled off.

"Well, I don't know," said Harriet Compton rather impatiently. "Maybe I only thought there must be one because I'm a cribbage nut myself. Maybe I read somewhere that Jason Cirak liked to play cribbage, too, and it stuck in my mind. There used to be a lot of stuff written about him back when he was a big name in films, you know. James—I mean Cirak—was a colorful personality."

"That's not what the Plummers call him. I do know there was publicity even after he and my mother were married, because Uncle Fred and Aunt Martha still haven't got over his dragging the Plummer name through the newspapers. I never got to read any of the articles, naturally."

"No, I don't suppose they kept scrapbooks. It's a shame, Jenny. You have a right to know both sides of the story. If you like, we might drive into Providence and see if they keep old periodical files at the main library there. Maybe we can find some stories about your father. And see if they say anything about cribbage," she added with a wry smile. "Not that it matters now."

"How do you know it doesn't? Maybe that cribbage board is the clue to the whole mystery." Jenny opened her father's desk and pulled the cribbage board out of its drawer. "Here it is. Does it suggest anything to you?"

Harriet Compton ran her fingers over the long strip of wood. "It's so worn." Her voice was almost a whisper. "I hadn't realized James was so old."

"He must have played on it for years and years." Jenny looked down at the age-stained board, its holes worn out of their serried regularity by countless movings of the metal pegs that marked the scoring. She'd wanted something like this. She'd hoped that somewhere in her father's house there'd be some keepsake he'd carried around with him through the years, in and out of whatever adventures had landed him at last in this made-over carriage house in a tiny Rhode Island village. And here it was, this piece of wood bored full of holes, rubbed to an antique sheen by the hands of Jason Cirak.

Or was it? Maybe the cribbage board wasn't even his, just one more bit of clutter that had been left behind when that old woman who'd been here before him died and was taken away to be buried. Maybe the thing meant nothing at all. So why was Harriet Compton poring over it so avidly, touching the holes, turning the board over and over in her competent hands, running her fingertips along the edges, which had been rounded by years of handling? Did she think that bit of hand-polished walnut could tell her who had been Jason Cirak's cribbage partner on that fatal night last March?

If the board held a secret, it had no way to tell. Harriet handed the thin, worn slab back to Cirak's daughter.

"Put it back where you found it, Jenny. We can't play on James's board. It belongs to a time that's over and done with forever."

After that, the gentle closing of a desk drawer and the snapping of applewood logs in the fireplace were the only sounds to be heard in the old carriage house. Two women, one older and one younger than either had realized herself to be until now, sat side by side, trapped by their thoughts inside an eagle's nest.

13:

It was Harriet Compton who broke the spell. "Well, that's that for today, as far as I'm concerned. I'm going to stick a few rollers in my hair and get ready for bed."

"All right. You get finished in the bathroom and I'll be along. I'm just going to rinse out these mugs."

Miss Compton was in the little guest room and Jenny tidying the kitchen when Lawrence MacRae came to the door carrying the matte-finished enlargement he'd promised Jenny.

"Sorry to come so late, but I didn't want to hurry the drying for fear of spoiling the print."

"That's all right," she assured him. "I didn't expect you to have it done this soon."

"I felt I owed you some kind of apology, Miss—is it still Plummer?"

"You'd better call me Jenny. Come in for a minute, won't you? It will give Sue Giles something to talk about. Aunt Harriet's probably got her curlers in by now, but she won't mind."

"Not a bit. Good evening, Larry." The older woman entered the living room with a silk scarf draped coiflike over her head. "Personal vanity has never been one of my failings, mainly because I've had nothing to be vain about."

"What are you talking about?" the photographer contradicted. "You'd have made a great fashion model if you'd ever wanted to. You've got the height, and the bones. In fact you'd be a terrific study right now against the dying fire, with that thing over your head, though I don't suppose you'd let me shoot it."

"On the contrary, I should be intensely flattered," said Miss Compton. "And I don't mind saying so because I notice you don't have a camera with you."

"Ah, but I do!"

MacRae whipped a tiny Minox out of his car coat pocket. "Mind sitting on the edge of that chair and leaning forward? I want to get your profile silhouetted in the light from the coals. Great! Oh, blast, I forgot I don't have superfast film in this thing. It'll have to be a time exposure. Is there anything around here I could use for a tripod?"

"Mean to say you don't have one of those in your coat pocket, too?" Jenny teased, fetching a step stool from the kitchen. "Will this do?"

"Perfect."

He steadied the miniature camera on top of the stool

and squinted through the viewfinder. "A little more forward. Good. Hold it for a second."

MacRae pressed the shutter release and eyed the second hand on his watch. "Okay, now face me just a little."

He took four or five more exposures, then lamented that he had no more film and put his camera away. "Where does this stool go, Jenny? I don't know if those shots will amount to anything. I'd like to try again with better equipment, if you'll pose for me, Miss Compton. I'm supposed to be doing a series on American faces for *Pictorial Magazine,* and you're a natural for it. You wouldn't mind, would you?"

"I'd be tickled silly. I was—somebody told me once I'd be good in pictures, but I thought it was only because he— liked me."

Why wouldn't he, whoever he'd been? Jenny was glad to see that MacRae's unexpected but obviously sincere admiration had been the perfect tonic for the somber mood Harriet Compton had been in a while ago. She didn't know why the older woman's happiness was so important to her, when they hardly knew each other. Surely there must be some tie of relationship, like the one Harriet had discovered with Elspeth Gillespie.

Or was that merely wishful thinking? She wanted Harriet to be family because Harriet was so exactly the kind of relative she'd needed all her life. Jenny had never been really accepted anywhere. She was too much a Cirak for the Plummers, too much a reminder of the cataclysmic error Marion had made on the one fateful occasion when she'd insisted on having her own way in the face of the family's objections. Furthermore, Marion herself had never, deep down, wanted Jenny. You couldn't stay the little girl of the family if you had a daughter of your own.

The kids Jenny had met and liked at school were never the kind Aunt Martha would have wanted coming to the house; so although she was naturally sociable, she'd wound up with the reputation of being a loner. Having one person in her life who'd at least have made an honest effort to understand her would have been a blessing beyond words. Harriet Compton was more than that. She knew without having to try. Was she that way with everyone?

Harriet had Lawrence MacRae nicely wound around her little finger already. He was telling her a funny story about having to take close-up photographs of a sea lion with herring halitosis, so that he could watch her face when she laughed. Jenny began to feel a bit out of it.

"Shall I put on the tea kettle?" she offered. "Here, Lawrence, let me do something about your coat."

"Most people call me Larry," he answered. "Don't bother. Just throw it down somewhere."

"I'm too house-proud for that."

The car coat was a good one, tailored of dark green corduroy. Its classic lines reminded Jenny of that blood-stained suede jacket. Not much liking the task, she went to the coat closet and hung MacRae's beside the one Harriet Compton had brought in her gold-mounted attaché case. It didn't take a tailor's eye to see that the two garments were exactly the same size.

14

"Nonsense, Jenny! That can't possibly be Larry's jacket."

"Why not? Because he thinks you're beautiful?" Cirak's daughter dumped the eggy frying pan into the sink and ran cold water over it. "I thought we were going by the facts."

"And the fact is that I'm ugly?" Aunt Harriet spooned gooseberry jam over her toast, as if she didn't care one way or the other.

"That's not what I mean, and you know it. The fact is that I compared his jacket with it, and they're exactly the same size and style."

"But what motive could Larry have to kill James?"

"How am I supposed to know? Maybe be found out my father was trifling with his grandmother's affections."

"Maybe he thought James was planning to pinch old

Colin's bagpipes. Jenny, you can't honestly believe an intelligent young man who's been around as much as Sue Giles claims Larry has would kill such a magnificent model as your father just to protect his grandmother's virtue? Did Elspeth Gillespie strike you as the helpless sort?"

"No, but I've been wrong before."

Jenny sat down and started eating her breakfast. "I don't want to suspect Larry any more than you do. He's not so bad once you get past the mustache. But that doesn't mean we can shut our eyes to the evidence, does it? I wish I'd given him the wrong jacket when he left, the way I did Greg Bauer night before last."

"You'd have been making a mistake if you did. Larry's no dope." Harriet buttered more toast and passed it over to Jenny. "Anyway, I can think of at least one other man not far from here who's almost the same height and build, and dresses even better."

An image of Larry and another tall, thinnish, nattily-garbed man shoving a sofa across the church vestry flashed into Jenny's mind. "So can I. Jack Firbelle."

"Too right, as an Australian client of mine used to say. Gooseberry jam?"

"Please."

Jenny's appetite was picking up. She wouldn't mind so much if the jacket turned out to be Jack Firbelle's. What business did he have dolling himself up like a male fashion model and letting his cousin go around like a walking ragbag? She said so.

"Yours is a God of justice and of wrath, I see," was Harriet Compton's only reply.

"What's that supposed to mean? Don't you think he deserves what's coming to him for being so ratty to Beth?"

"How do I know what he deserves? Whatever it is, he'll get it sooner or later. People always do, so why fret about it? Furthermore, kindly remember that it's never safe to judge by appearances."

"Yes, Auntie dear. I adore you when you go all sententious. More coffee?"

"Thanks, Jenny. I'm glad you don't mind my preaching. I used to do so much of it that I can't get out of the habit, even now when I have nobody left to preach to."

"You have me." Jenny stopped pouring. "Aunt Harriet, you're not just—just going back to Baltimore, are you?"

"Don't you want me to? Wouldn't you rather see me fade away, now that I've brought you a fresh lot of worries?"

"Don't be ridiculous. You haven't brought me any trouble I didn't have before." Jenny decided she'd better set down the coffeepot before she poured its contents all over the table. "Aunt Harriet, I—I don't think I could bear to have you walk out of my life the way my father did."

"I don't think I could do it, Jenny." Harriet Compton laid her knife and fork with painstaking exactness across her empty plate. "I guess it's time I told you something."

"I know." Jenny recalled something else: those long, loving hands fondling the wornout cribbage board. "You knew my father, didn't you?"

"I was the woman your mother wouldn't let him marry."

"Oh."

This was the one step Jenny's intuition hadn't been able to take.

"Rather a shock, isn't it?" Harriet Compton tried to force a smile. "I'm not exactly your classic figure of romance, am I? I understand your mother was a very pretty woman."

"She still is."

Except for the peevish droop to the mouth formed by eighteen years of lamenting that her husband had left her for another.

"I didn't take your father away from you, Jenny. That's the God's honest truth, no matter what you've heard. I didn't meet James until—well, until after he'd had his last flop and started calling himself James instead of Jason. That must have been when you were about seven years old. I never even knew there'd been a child until five years later."

"How did he ever get around to telling you?"

"It happened pretty much by accident, if you want the truth. I used to subscribe to a lot of out-of-town newspapers so that I could go bloodhounding through the financial pages. James was browsing through them one Sunday morning, sprawled out on the sofa with his shoes off and his shirt half-unbuttoned. James never stayed properly dressed for long if he could help it. He told me that was one of the reasons he couldn't stand living with your mother. She wouldn't let him be comfortable."

Harriet caught herself. "I'm sorry, Jenny. I didn't mean to get on that subject. Anyway, James was scrabbling through the papers and throwing the pages all over the floor as he always did, when he suddenly yelled, 'Good

God, Hat, look at this! That's my daughter.' You'd won first prize in a school essay contest, and they'd run your picture with a little squib about your being the daughter of Jason Cirak, the late producer. James thought it was hilarious that they'd written up the article as if he were dead. I didn't think it was so funny, myself."

The accountant cleared her throat. "Jenny, I was forty-one years old when I met James. He was the first man I'd ever loved. Until then, I'd been too preoccupied with family problems to think about romance for myself. The trite old story of the self-sacrificing spinster with an invalid mother to support. Any woman who can't fight her way out of that box is either a fool or a self-made martyr."

Her lips tightened. "Mother was gone by then, and I was left alone to realize I'd spent all those years living somebody else's life instead of my own. When James told me he loved me and wanted me, I can't tell you what it meant. I even had a wild hope that if we married right away, I might still be able to bear his child. Well, we couldn't so we didn't."

"Thanks to my mother."

Then Marion Plummer Cirak had paid back her husband's new love even more savagely than she'd realized. Was that what constituted justice?

"I don't know, Jenny. I'm not blaming your mother. In a way, James queered his own pitch. She might have given him the divorce if he hadn't been dumb enough to tell her why he wanted it. Who's to say he didn't mean things to turn out as they did? Subconsciously, I think James was scared stiff of getting himself involved in another wife-

and-family situation because he'd made such a mess of the first one.''

She smiled wistfully and shook her well-coifed head. "What James wanted was to be babied himself. My maternal urges found plenty of outlet, believe me. For a long time I thought James himself was enough; but when I found out he actually had a daughter living, it all welled up again. I wanted you, Jenny. I wanted to take care of you, help you choose your clothes, tie your hair ribbons, cook your breakfast. I wondered how you'd talk, what color you'd choose for your bedroom wallpaper, all sorts of foolish things. I cut that picture out of the paper and carried it around in my wallet. I had it with me the day James and I finally flew to Haiti and got him a quickie divorce so that we could be married, after it was too late to matter much one way or the other. James Compton, it says on the license. Compton was my name, you see, and James had gotten used to being addressed as Mr. Compton when he was staying at my place.''

"So you're my stepmother! And—you're not making it up about the picture?''

"No, Jenny. It's still on my dressing table back in Baltimore. There didn't seem to be any point in bringing it with me this time.''

15 ❧

"All these years. I can't believe it." Jenny shook her head, then emitted a little snort of laughter. "I hope I wasn't too much of a disappointment to you."

"You're everything I expected you'd be. Of course I'll admit I already knew a lot about you. I've kept track of you as best I could without giving myself away and making trouble for you with the Plummers. I even went so far as to hire private detectives to spy on them and make sure you were being adequately taken care of. James thought I was crazy."

"I can imagine." Her mouth felt dry.

"It's not that you didn't matter to him, Jenny," her stepmother pleaded. "James knew Marion's family, that's all. If he hadn't been sure the Plummers would look after you, he'd never have abandoned you."

"Do you honestly believe that?"

Harriet Compton looked her new stepdaughter squarely in the eyes. "Jenny, I can't lie to you any more. I simply don't know whether I believe it or not. James was a fascinating, adorable man, and I loved him as I've never loved anybody else in my life, but I never shut my eyes to the fact that he couldn't be trusted the length of this room."

Jenny shifted her eyes. "So Uncle Fred was right."

"No, James wasn't a crook, if that's what you're getting at. He never stole a penny, in the strict sense of the word. He hated responsibility and loved to make a splash, so he needed lots of money. He couldn't endure the tedium of a steady job for more than a week or two at a time, so he lived by his wits."

"What's that supposed to mean?

"With James, it could mean anything. For instance, he once took a job running a mimeograph machine. That was after he'd faced the fact that he was washed up in films. Anyway, his second night on the job, he stayed overtime and ran off ten thousand copies of a chain letter. You know what those are, I presume?"

"Those idiotic messages you're supposed to make ump-teen copies of and send along to other people so the trolls won't get you. Aunt Martha has a nutty neighbor who's always passing them on to her. But there's no money involved."

"That's because asking for money in chain letters is now illegal, thanks partly to James. It wasn't, when he got his big idea. What he did was to sign six different names and addresses at the bottom of his letter, explaining that the receiver was to send a dollar to the top name on the list, then make six copies of the letter, dropping the name he'd sent the dollar to and adding his or her own name at the bottom of the list. By the time the sender's name worked its way to the top, the six receivers would each have sent the letter to six more, and so on. All in all, everybody was supposed to receive a total of $46,656, which wouldn't be a bad return on a dollar investment, you have to admit."

"But at that rate, you'd soon run out of names," Jenny protested.

"How right you are, but you'd be surprised how many people didn't think of that."

"Whose names did Father use?"

"His own, naturally. He rented post office boxes or accommodation addresses in six different places under six different aliases. Then he sent out his ten thousand letters at random all over the country, taking names and addresses from telephone books at the public library. Postage was much lower then, so it didn't take any great investment to launch his scheme. He'd made it all back by the end of the first week."

"But surely the whole ten thousand didn't reply?"

"Oh, no. Some were too lazy, I suppose, and some realized the flaws in James's arithmetic. I doubt if a single chain out of the ten thousand stayed intact for long. That's why they were ruled a violation of postal regulations, because they promised more than could logically be delivered. But by the time that ruling came through, James's six names were long gone from the lists, and he was sitting pretty on a pile of dollars."

"Didn't he know what he'd done was wrong?"

"James didn't see it that way. He argued that everybody'd been given a sporting chance to make money, which was all he'd given himself in the first place, and that nobody could lose more than one dollar plus postage. I'm sure he never felt a single twinge of conscience about what he'd done. James did have a pretty accommodating conscience, I must admit."

Harriet Compton started to laugh. "Some of his escapades were funny, like the Kvizitsia episode. James happened to wander into a little antique shop on Third Avenue in New York where he saw this unspeakable blob of an old oil painting. He was standing there, drinking in the exquisite awfulness of it, as he described it to me later, when a woman dripping mink and diamonds came in. Seeing him staring at the painting, she came over and started looking, too. James was never what you'd call shy, so he remarked, 'Perfect, isn't it?'

" 'Superb!' the woman gushed. 'Er—I'm afraid the artist's name escapes me for the moment.'

" 'That, madam, is a real Kvizitsia,' James informed her. That's a Yiddish word that had come up pretty often while they were filming *The Refugees*. It means inquisition, literally, but it's used to refer to anything that's a complete and utter disaster. The antique dealer knew, of course. James said the man was killing himself in the background laughing, but this woman in the mink looked ever so impressed.

" 'What do you think he's asking for it?'

" 'I've been wondering that, myself. Nothing like what it's worth, I'd expect.' James thought that was a fair enough statement, because the dealer must surely be asking something, and the painting wasn't worth a plugged nickel. By this time, the woman's tongue was practically hanging out.

" 'Do you plan to make him an offer?' she asked.

"James put on a big act. 'Well, you don't find something like this every day.' That was true enough, too!

" 'I'll say five hundred,' she told him.

" 'My dear lady!' said James.

" 'A thousand.'

" 'Two?'

" 'Two-five.'

" 'Three?'

" 'Four thousand, and that's my final offer,' the woman snapped.

"With that, James gave her a gallant bow as only he knew how to do. He was an awful ham, Jenny. 'It would be most ungentlemanly of me to outbid so charming and determined a connoisseur,' he told her.

"So believe it or not, the woman opened her pocketbook right then and there and forked over four thousand-dollar bills to the dealer. James flagged her down a taxi, helped her into it with her genuine Kvizitsia, then went back into the shop and held out his hand. The dealer plunked two of the thousand-dollar bills into it, they both had a good laugh, and James went strolling on his merry way."

Jenny couldn't help laughing, too. "I suppose anybody that rich and that gullible is asking to be taken."

"When the heavens rain manna upon you, don't put up an umbrella. Hold out a tub. That's what your father would have said. James never pulled the same one twice. He didn't have to."

"So that's how he made his fortune."

"Not so you'd notice it, young woman. James couldn't keep a cent in his pocket long enough for it to burn a hole through. I'll admit your initial capital came from some rather unusual sources, but the profits on it were legitimate enough. As soon as I found out James had a daughter, I made up my mind you were going to be properly provided for, Plummers or no Plummers. From then on, whenever James came home bragging that he'd hauled off another little deal, I made him fork over half of whatever he had on him, right then and there. That money went into what we called our Jenny Fund.

"I got your portfolio started with some good, safe municipal bonds. After I'd built up a decent backlog of blue-chip securities, I began to speculate. Maybe it was because I was investing for you instead of myself, but everything I touched paid off. I'm not denying James and I did all right, too, but you came first. When the money started to pile up, I established that trust, not to beat the tax man as your Uncle Fred no doubt suspected, but to screen the connection between you and your father."

"Why did you do that, Aunt Harriet?"

"I had to, Jenny. I never knew when James might stumble over that fine line he drew between right and wrong and land himself in the soup."

"Which he finally did," Jenny said bitterly.

"Jenny, I hope you're not blaming me for what happened. I never tried to keep James tied to my apron strings. He was a born roamer, but I figured he'd always come back sooner or later. If he didn't, that was my tough luck. I'd taken him for what he was, not for a lump of silly putty I could squeeze into any shape I wanted."

Harriet rubbed a long-fingered hand over her eyes. "Loving somebody isn't all moonlight and roses and splitting up as soon as the violins start playing a little bit off-key. It's damned hard work, if you want the truth. Anyway, that's beside the point. As to why he was killed, I'm sure it wasn't because he'd got involved in anything crooked for the sake of the money. We were financially secure by then, and he knew it. Nor can I see him deliberately putting himself in danger. James liked the fun of the game, whatever the game might be, but he was fond of his own handsome skin, too."

"Then what was he doing in Meldrum? Can you tell me that?"

"I'm surprised you haven't guessed. James wanted to make a comeback as Jason Cirak. He'd been talking a lot about the grand old days when he was a famous producer, how he'd been wasting his time, frittering away his talents these past years, and all that jazz. He'd gotten an idea for another film, and he was using Meldrum as a testing board, manipulating people to see how they'd react."

"But you can't do that to human beings," Jenny protested.

"James could. He treated the world the way a baby treats its teddy bear. People were his toys. He wasn't nasty about it, of course. If they wouldn't play the way he wanted the game to go, he'd simply go off and find himself a new set of playmates."

"Then since he hadn't left Meldrum, he must have

thought the game was still going his way," said Jenny slowly. "Only—it wasn't."

This wasn't easy, having to accept a father who'd used a planet for his playpen and a stepmother who'd never known her before but had cared enough to build a future for her. Harriet had done what her father hadn't had the stability or her mother the energy to do. If she'd had to choose among them, which would she have picked?

"No, it wasn't." Harriet Compton was sitting with her head bowed, as if in farewell to the rover she'd managed somehow to stay in love with all these years. "Maybe a sudden death wasn't the worst thing that could have happened to your father, Jenny. He'd never have made it back as Jason Cirak. He'd left the screen a failure. He'd been away too long, and he was out of step with what's being done today. And James would have hated being an old man. From Peter Pan to Pantaloon with nothing in between—" She brushed away the years with a sweep of her long-boned hand.

"But it left me so terribly alone, Jenny. I even missed the phone bills." She managed a wry chuckle.

"James had a habit of calling collect from wherever he happened to be and talking for hours. He'd phoned me only the night before he died, full of beans and dropping mysterious hints about how well the new project was going. He wanted me to meet him in New York the following weekend so he could tell me all about it. That wasn't unusual. James often expected me to charge off somewhere or other at a moment's notice. He never liked being separated from me too long. I didn't like it much, either."

She stopped for a moment to get her voice back under control. "And two days later I got a copy of the Meldrum *Times*. I'd started taking the local paper when James moved here. I figured he'd be in it sooner or later, but I hadn't expected a front-page story saying he was dead."

There was another pause. "I couldn't do much myself for fear of its reflecting on you. As you know, he'd been passing as James Cox, a childless widower. So I sent Joe Delorio up here to clear out his personal possessions and had the body shipped back to Baltimore as soon as the police would release it. Then we had a private funeral, just my Jimmy and me and a few old friends."

Harriet blew her nose on her napkin and wiped away the tears. "He's buried in our family plot down there, next to my twin brother, who died when we were young. I always thought it was a pity Harry couldn't have known James. After that, there wasn't much else I could do. I was furious at that stupid verdict, of course, but I hesitated to stick my own oar in until I heard through our lawyers that you wanted to come here and take possession of the house. I had to act then. How did I know you weren't walking straight into whatever situation had caused your father's death?"

"But that suede jacket? Where did that come from? Was it—"

"No, it wasn't James's. I picked it up at a thrift shop, if you want to know. It was an idea James had had once about how to get his foot in somebody's door for some reason or other. He was always tossing off these gems and then forgetting all about them; but I have a long memory. Anyway, I was coming back from the lawyer's office,

racking my brain about what to do, and there was the
jacket in the window of a second-hand clothing store, so
I went in and bought it. Somebody'd spilled grease or
something down the front. I decided blood would be more
artistic, so I slopped a piece of raw liver on top of the
stains. Not a very nice thing to do, but I wanted to scare
you into either clearing out or letting me stay. You were
all I had left, you see."

Jenny reached over and squeezed her stepmother's hand.
"Couldn't you have just come?"

"Barged in here and said, 'How do you do, I'm your
stepmother?' I don't have that kind of nerve, Jenny. There
was too much at risk. You looked enough like your
father that I hoped I could arouse your interest without
making you suspicious of me by using his own method."
She smiled. "The wrapping came off a present James had
sent me from here the week before he died. It was a pink
plush kangaroo with a bottle of aspirin and a lovely gold
pillbox set with pearls tucked into the pouch. I could
have brought the kangaroo instead, I suppose, but it
wouldn't have done the trick as well, would it?"

Jenny shook her head. "No, the jacket was—convincing.
But if you knew it was a fake, why did you let me go
through that business about trying it on Greg Bauer?"

"Mere corroborative detail, as Pooh-Bah would say, designed to lend credence to a pretty thin story. But you can
see now why the jacket couldn't be young MacRae's. Or
Jack Firbelle's, for that matter. I suppose we might as
well get rid of it. Maybe you'd as soon get rid of me, too,
now that you know how I've tricked you."

Jenny shoved back her chair and ran around the table.

"How can you think that? You can't run out on me. I'm your daughter!"

All of a sudden they were having a real, satisfying weep together, Jenny's head pressed against her stepmother's shoulder, and Harriet's cheek resting on the thick black hair that felt so much like Jason Cirak's. After a while, the older woman picked up a fresh paper napkin and wiped away her tears. "Well, this isn't getting much done."

"It is so," Jenny snuffled. "It's the most important thing that ever happened."

Harriet gave her another squeeze. "I stand corrected, Jenny, my own. I've wanted this for so long. I never dreamed it would happen this way."

Jenny took another napkin and mopped at the face she'd inherited from Jason Cirak along with his money and his wife. "What difference does it make how? The big thing is, it's happened."

16 🌹🌹🌹

They were calming their emotions and practicing their mother-daughter relationship by washing the dishes together when Beth arrived with another bunch of chrysanthemums and a note from Aunt Marguerite. Mrs. Firbelle hoped Jenny and her aunt would drop over at seven that evening for a simple family dinner.

She's not my aunt, Jenny wanted to answer. She's my stepmother; and I'm not Jenny Plummer but Jenny Cirak. And I don't want to come to your house because I don't like the way it feels over there.

But she couldn't. She didn't dare go back to being Jenny Cirak until she'd found out who or what had killed her father. And she must go to the Firbelles' because if she let herself be scared away, she'd never learn what she had to know. She sat down at the desk and wrote a polite acceptance on a piece of the late Jason Cirak's writing paper.

"There you are, Beth, and thanks so much for coming. I suppose you'll be off to the rummage sale pretty soon."

"Oh yes. I'll just take your note back to Aunt Marguerite, then run right over to the church. We're having a chowder luncheon, and that will mean a lot of extra work. I don't suppose you two would care to attend? It's only a dollar fifty per person."

"At that price, we can't afford to miss it. What do you say, Aunt Harriet?"

"Sounds great to me. Have you any tickets with you, Beth?"

"No, but I'll make sure they save a couple for you at the door. We're hoping for a big turnout. We'll be serving from half-past eleven till two o'clock. We hope some of the husbands will come since it's Saturday. Getting the men to participate is always a problem."

"Your cousin Jack will be there, I suppose?" Jenny said.

"Yes, he's going to set up the chairs and so forth. Jack's not a bad helper if you prod him hard enough," Beth admitted. "I'll be looking for you, then."

"We'll probably drop in sometime around noon."

"And in the meantime," Harriet suggested after Beth had left her with her note, "I move we give this joint a real scrubdown. I'm itching to get at those corners nobody could clean while the rooms were so full of junk. James would never throw out a stick, of course. I wouldn't be surprised if he'd lugged in half the stuff himself. James had a positive passion for clutter."

"I do love it when you run on about Father that way," Jenny said. "You make him sound so human."

"Why not? He was." Harriet made a little sound, halfway between a chuckle and a sigh. "I'm going to talk about him a lot, Jenny, partly because I want you to know him as he was, and partly because it makes me feel better. I've never had anybody before to whom I could really talk about James."

She gave her stepdaughter a quick hug, then grabbed the new vacuum cleaner they'd bought on their shopping expedition and attacked the grubby floors with the zest of a ten-year-old.

The hard work did them both good and didn't hurt the carriage house, either. By half-past twelve they'd gotten themselves showered and changed and left the spic-and-span house.

"Let's walk," Jenny suggested. "My lungs need the air. I'll bet we inhaled dust that hadn't been disturbed for fifty years."

"Longer than that. I'm game." Harriet fell into stride, her long legs making quick work of the not-very-well-tended sidewalk.

"The question now," said Jenny, as if she were picking up a suspended conversation, "is what clues we have to Father's death? Without the jacket, that is."

"None at all," said Harriet Compton. "And that's what worries me. We don't know what we're looking for, or why. All we can do is keep our eyes and ears open. I worry about you here, Jenny. We have to know what happened, before we can be sure you're safe."

"But no one knows he was my father."

"Doesn't matter. It could have been that casual prowler, who might return—might even have been the person you saw the other night. Or this house might hold something someone wants and is willing to murder for. Though, whoever it was seems to have made no attempt to find anything the night James was killed."

"Maybe Beth and Jack came too soon after."

"No, I think not. Beth said the body was stiff. But something else could have scared the killer off."

Jenny shuddered. She hadn't really considered herself in danger, though she'd been afraid the night she saw the prowler. After, she'd assumed it was Lawrence MacRae. But maybe not!

As they neared the church, they met quite a number of women and children, plus a fair sprinkling of men. "Beth's getting her turnout," Harriet observed, changing the subject. "She's a good organizer."

"Then why doesn't she get out and organize herself a job?" said Jenny.

"Maybe Aunt Whoozis thinks it would be demeaning. Anyway, running a church social once a year and putting in a steady nine-to-five fifty weeks in a row are two very different kettles of fish. Speaking of fish, I hope they haven't run out of chowder. It smells divine, and I'm starving."

They had nothing to worry about. Their tickets were at the door as promised, and Jack Firbelle was on the *qui vive* to escort them to places of honor beside the minister's wife, apologizing because his mother couldn't be there to bestow the yet greater luster of her presence. She was probably at home deciding whether that impromptu little dinner should have five or six courses, Jenny thought nastily.

The chowder was excellent, even though it had been made Rhode Island style. Fish chowder with tomatoes in it would have sent Aunt Martha Plummer into a swoon and Uncle Fred raging from the hall, which made Jenny enjoy it all the more. The crackers were crisply toasted, the apple pie homemade, there was real cream for the coffee. The Gileses and some of the people Jenny had met at their party were present. So were Elspeth Gillespie and Larry MacRae. They all made a point of coming over to say hello and to hope the new neighbors were having a good time. They were, until the fight broke out.

Pamela and Greg Bauer were sitting at the next table with another youngish couple and the plump woman Jenny remembered as Cousin Daisy. There were several children in their party, and while the parents dawdled over their coffee, the youngsters got up and began sky-larking around the tables. Since no church social is complete without a troop of boys and girls milling about, nobody paid much attention to them until the oldest Bauer, a boy about twelve years old who'd inherited his father's burly build and didn't yet know how to handle it, came nose-to-nose with a teenage girl carrying a loaded tray. The amateur waitress was nervous, young Bauer was clumsy, and Bill Giles had the bad luck to be sitting where the chowder landed.

For a man his age, Bill could move fast. He was out of his chair and attacking the miscreant almost before the chowder stopped dripping.

"You young punk!"

The Bauer boy began to stammer out an apology, but Giles refused to listen. He slapped the youngster hard, then began shaking him savagely.

"Hey, cut that out!"

Greg Bauer tried to intervene. "Lay off the kid, Bill. It was an accident. He didn't mean to do it."

"You want a punch in the mouth?" Giles hurled the son halfway across the table and turned on the father.

Greg was almost twice Bill's size and probably twenty years younger. The situation should have been absurd. But there was nothing funny about this blind, senseless rage. Even when Lawrence MacRae got Giles in an arm-lock and wrenched him away, he kept threshing blows at the target he could no longer reach.

"Sue," screamed Greg's wife Pamela, "can't you stop him?"

"I don't dare," Sue moaned. "If I interfere, he only gets worse."

"What do you mean?" said Harriet Compton. "Does he often act like this?"

"I never know what will set him off." Sue was crying now. "He's like a wild animal when he gets mad. I'm scared of him."

"Answer me. How often does it happen? Is this something new, or has he always been this bad?"

"It's—just lately. He was always so good-natured. Oh, I'm so ashamed!"

"Don't be an idiot. Can't you see the man is sick?"

Harriet took command. "Larry, you and Greg get him out to your wagon. Don't let go of him for one second. Mr. Firbelle, stand by to help if they need you. Knock him cold if you can't control him any other way, but for God's sake don't hit too hard."

"I'll drive," said Jenny. "Larry's got his hands full. Where's the nearest mental hospital?"

"You're not taking him there!" shrieked Bill's wife.

"Sue, you've got to understand that your husband is ill."

"Then take him to a doctor. Let me take him to Dr. O'Hare. He's just down the street."

"Very well, if you insist."

Jenny knew better than to waste time arguing with a hysterical woman. Sue was beside herself now, and her loud sobs were only driving her husband to greater fury.

"Come along if you must, but for goodness' sake try to control yourself." Harriet Compton took one of Sue's arms, the minister's wife took the other. Together they marched her out of the room.

Beth Firbelle was cowering by the door, her air of efficiency completely shattered by this ugly turn of affairs. Jenny stopped for a second to speak to her.

"Beth, get a mop and clean up that mess over there. Carry on as though nothing had happened."

"That's right, Beth. You've worked so hard. We mustn't let this spoil your sale." Jack Firbelle showed an unexpected streak of compassion by slipping his arm around his cousin's shoulders. "Come on, I'll help."

By now several other men were volunteering their services to Larry and Greg, so Jack was probably of more use at the sale anyway. Luckily Bill had turned sullen by the time they got him into the car, only muttering threats and curses and making an occasional attempt to wrench away from his captors. Better still, Dr. O'Hare was at home, though none too happy about being dragged away from his lunch. He took one look at the patient, barked a few questions at Sue, laid her out in lavender for not having had sense enough to call him sooner, and pumped a tranquilizer into Bill's arm.

"There, that ought to keep him quiet till you get him to the hospital. No sense in my coming, he needs a neurological specialist. I'll phone to let them know he's on his way. Sue, you get yourself home to bed. Take one of these capsules and lie down."

"I ought to stay with Bill. He's my husband, after all," she sobbed.

"You can't do him any good by wailing all over him, and it's not going to help you any, either. Greg, take care of Sue. Get Pamela to stay with her till she quiets down. Larry should be able to manage Bill with that dose he's got inside him, if these two ladies don't mind going along to drive the car."

"We'll manage," said Harriet Compton. "Go with Greg, Sue. We'll let you know as soon as there's anything to report."

"But what am I going to tell the neighbors?"

"Tell them your husband's had a seizure and has gone to the hospital for treatment," roared Dr. O'Hare. "For the cat's sake, Sue, this isn't the dark ages. It's no more disgraceful to have something wrong with your head than with your foot. Offhand, I'd say Bill's got some hardening of the arteries that's affecting the blood supply to the brain, but we'll know better after they've run an EEG on him. Now beat it, all of you, and let me eat my lunch."

Greg Bauer helped Larry MacRae get Bill back into

the station wagon, then they dropped Sue at her house and drove to the church so Greg could pick up his car and his wife. At last Jenny turned out on the Providence road.

It was a silent ride. Jenny had never handled such a large car before and had to concentrate on her driving. MacRae and Miss Compton had their hands full with Giles, whom even the massive tranquilizing shot had not fully subdued. They were all relieved when the impressive sprawl of the mental hospital loomed into sight; gladder still when the formalities were over, their troublesome charge was in capable hands, and they were at last free to head back to Meldrum.

17

"I move we stop for coffee."

Harriet Compton's words were almost the first any of them had spoken since they'd left Bill at the hospital. "I don't know about you two, but I feel the need."

"So do I."

Jenny had gratefully turned the wheel of the big wagon over to Larry for the return drive. She was huddled down beside him now, very small inside her new suede coat, the one she'd wondered if she could ever bring herself to wear again after she'd seen the bloodstains on that other suede jacket, which was still hanging in her hall closet but would never give her the horrors again.

MacRae glanced down at her and grinned. "I like you better without your hair."

"Aunt Harriet made me put that wig in the rummage

sale," Jenny admitted. "It was supposed to be a disguise."

"All it did was accentuate your resemblance to your father, by making you look older."

"Well, how was I to know what my father looked like?"

"And how was I to know you didn't know? Come on, I'll buy the coffee."

He turned in at the next coffee shop they came to and helped them out of the wagon. Jenny noticed how tired he looked.

"You must be exhausted, Larry. You were sweet to take all this trouble for Bill Giles."

He shrugged. "Oh, I'm everybody's errand boy when I'm in Meldrum. That's what comes of not having a steady job. People think you've got all the time in the world just because you don't have to turn up at an office every day."

"I daresay if some of your neighbors had to follow you around when you're on assignment, they'd think twice about interfering with your leisure," Harriet Compton observed. "You must wish you'd been anywhere but at that chowder luncheon this noon."

"You can say that again." He sighed. "I always did think Sue Giles had the brains of a hen, but how she could have been stupid enough to let that situation go on is beyond me. Bill might have done some real damage to the Bauer kid, slinging him around like that. What if he'd banged his head on the corner of the table, or slashed an artery on a broken dish? Bill could have killed somebody in one of those blind rages."

A sickening thought flashed through Jenny's mind. "Maybe he did," she whispered.

"Jenny, what do you mean?"

"Aunt Harriet, do you remember my telling you I thought Sue was scared about something that day she was over having tea with us? What if it's because she either thinks or knows it was her husband who killed my father?"

"That doesn't make sense," MacRae argued. "I didn't mean—"

"Oh, yes, you did. Why doesn't it make sense? Did it make any sense for Bill to go after that poor kid the way he did? Did it make any sense for him to attack Greg, who could have wiped him out with one good swing, when Greg was only trying to protect his own child from getting beaten up for no good reason? Why even talk about sense when a man's in that state? If Bill's all that mentally disturbed, he could have gone wild and killed my father over some foolish thing."

MacRae stirred the coffee the waitress had shoved in front of them. "Like what, for instance?"

"How do I know? Maybe a cribbage game."

MacRae quit stirring. "Why did you say that?"

"I don't know. I haven't the faintest idea of whether Bill Giles has ever played cribbage in his life. My father used to, that's all."

The photographer grunted and shook his head. "Bill plays cribbage down at the fire station four or five nights every week, and he always gets sore as a boil if he loses."

"James, on the other hand, was a gallant loser but an insufferable winner," said Harriet Compton.

"So Bill lost a game, popped his cork, and beaned Cox over the head with the cribbage board?" MacRae shook his head. "Cox was no pushover. I'd have had to see that one to believe it."

"Too bad you didn't. Where were you the night Mr. Cox was killed? In Meldrum, by any chance?"

"No, as it happened, I was at Logan Airport on standby, trying to catch a flight to Paris."

And Logan was in Boston, perhaps an hour and a half's drive from Meldrum.

"How did you find out about the murder?"

"What makes you so sure it was murder?" he shot back. "You've heard the official verdict, haven't you?"

"Official horsefeathers." Harriet Compton snorted. "Somebody did a spot of arm-twisting over that case, and you can't tell me they didn't. Who put the fix on, do you know?"

MacRae shrugged. "If I knew, do you think I'd have kept a story like that under my hat? As I told you, I wasn't around when it happened."

"But surely you've heard people talking about it since you got back," Harriet insisted.

"No, as a matter of fact there's been surprisingly little said about Cox, at least when I've been around. Maybe that's because Sue Giles is generally the center of all the town gossip, and I can see why she'd keep quiet if there was any chance Bill might be involved. I guess I didn't want to hear you on that one, Jenny. Bill used to fix my bike for me when I was a kid. He was always such an easy-going guy, it's no wonder Sue managed to cover up his temper fits. But it's not only Sue who doesn't want to talk about Cox. Even my grandmother steers clear of that subject. You must have noticed that yesterday. She just makes some kind of remark about what a gr-rand man he was, then turns you on to something else."

"One can understand why," said Harriet Compton with a knowing look. "I gathered from what little she did say yesterday that there was a good deal more than mere neighborliness between them."

"My grandmother and Cox?" yelped the photographer. "At her age?"

"Her age is probably pretty darn close to my age, young man, so watch your tongue. Furthermore, I wish you'd kindly tell me where you kids get the idea that any-body over forty is ready for the glue factory."

"Okay, if you say so. I suppose anything's possible."

MacRae began to laugh. "Jenny, how about that? If my grandmother had married your father, you'd have been my aunt."

"Perish the thought! I've got more relatives than I need already. Aunt Harriet, do you think that's why Mrs. Gillespie was so positive Father wasn't serious about Mrs. Firbelle? He wouldn't have gone so far as to hand them both the same line, would he?"

"Short of actually marrying either of them, which he knew darn well he couldn't get away with, I can't imagine James boggling at anything that would help his game along. For all I know, he was making a play for every woman in Meldrum."

MacRae's eyes narrowed. "And what exactly was his game, may I ask?"

"James was a—he'd written a few screen plays years ago, and he had an idea for another. He was here gather-ing material for a story line he wanted to develop. We'd—

happened to get together in Baltimore before he came, and he'd told me that much. He didn't go into details as to how he planned to go about it, but it looks to me as if he'd cast himself as a sort of small-town Don Juan to see what different women's reactions would be."

"If that's what he was up to, he deserved what he got."

"What right have you to say that?" Jenny blazed. "You didn't know him."

"I thought you didn't, either."

"That's enough," snapped Harriet Compton. "Larry, you only know what you saw of James, and Jenny only knows what she's been told. Neither of you has a right to judge him, and that's not what's important now anyway."

"Then what is?"

"Finding out who killed him and why, because Jenny isn't safe until we know."

"Jenny?" said MacRae blankly. "What's her father's death got to do with her?"

"Larry, can't you get it through your skull that we just don't know? We don't accept the accident theory; and misadventure doesn't mean a darn thing, as you must realize yourself. We assume James was killed, either on the spur of the moment or as a result of a murder plot. If it was because of something he had, then Jenny may have inherited both the thing itself and the threat that goes with it. If it was on account of something he did, there may be dangerous repercussions for her."

"Why should that be?"

"Why shouldn't it? Think of the possibilities, Larry. Suppose, for instance, you took a picture of a group of people, just a random shot with no regard to the actual persons in it. Now, suppose that in the group there happened to be a criminal who'd gone to a lot of trouble to provide himself with an alibi that was supposed to show he couldn't have been where you now possessed visual proof that he was. How safe do you think you'd be unless he was able to get the film away from you before you managed to have it developed?"

MacRae shrugged. "I see your point. I could get bumped off and never know why."

"Exactly. And James bought this house furnished, when it had been standing idle ever since that old Mrs. Brady, I believe her name was, died. We don't know what may have been going on here all that time. All we know is that James didn't stay alive long after he moved in. We don't know if whatever may or may not have been in the works here has been resumed. We do know Jenny has seen one prowler near the place."

"I did, you know," said Jenny quietly. "At first I thought it was you, but now I'm sure it was someone else. And I do get—feelings about people. I can't explain them, either, but they happen. I wasn't trying to scare Mrs. Firbelle that night. I was scared myself, if you want to know. And you weren't exactly helpful."

The photographer flushed as red as his mustache. "You don't have to remind me. Jenny, I'm not asking you to forgive me, but try to look at it from my point of view. I knew your father was hanging around my grandmother, and I get feelings, too. I didn't like what I felt when I saw them together. It never occurred to me that he might be—well, courting her. To tell you the truth, I thought he was after her money. I was expecting him to try selling her some phony oil stock or something like that."

"James happened to be a wealthy man," said Harriet Compton stiffly, "and he was not in the habit of robbing widows."

"Yes, but Larry wouldn't know that," Jenny argued, rather to her own surprise. "After all, Father was up to something, even if it wasn't anything dishonest—or not what he'd consider dishonest, anyway. And looking prosperous is part of a confidence man's stock in trade, isn't it? I don't see where that was such an unreasonable mistake for Larry to make. You can't blame him for being concerned about his grandmother, can you? So I suppose when I turned up looking just like my father and trying to make the neighbors think I knew nothing about him— which happened to be more or less true, though Larry wouldn't have believed that, either—it must have looked as if I were in Meldrum to carry on the family business. Is that what happened, Larry?"

"Pretty much," he admitted. "I should have known better."

"You probably would have, if I hadn't worn that stupid wig and that slinky purple dress."

"You never told me about the slinky purple dress, Jenny," said Harriet Compton, who seemed to have recovered her good humor.

"I was too ashamed."

"Maybe they'll have another rummage sale," Larry consoled her. "All right, so where are we? You told Mrs. Firbelle she was in danger."

"No, I didn't. I said there was danger around her."

"Same thing, isn't it?"

"Not necessarily. Maybe—do you suppose I was getting some kind of hunch about my father? Maybe somebody killed him because he was stringing her along as well as Mrs. Gillespie, and this other person got jealous. Mrs. Firbelle doesn't have any old boyfriends hanging around, does she?"

"Not so you'd notice it," Larry answered. "Frankly, I can see somebody plotting to kill Mrs. Firbelle a lot easier than I could believe anybody'd want to marry her. She has the personality of a cobra, if you ask me. As for her money, you just have to look at that niece of hers to see how freely she throws it around. So let's suppose your presentiment, or whatever you call it, was true. Somebody was planning to bump off Ma Firbelle and decided to kill James Cox first because Cox was paying too much attention to her and getting in the way. Or maybe Cox realized what was in the wind and tried to warn off the would-be killer or something. He was a bright guy, as I probably don't have to tell you."

"He was bright enough not to go messing around with a murderer," Harriet Compton objected.

"All right, I won't argue the point. What I mean is that the prowler Jenny saw would hardly have been after Mrs. Firbelle. Why would he back off for six months after he'd killed Cox, and then appear again on the same night Jenny had warned Mrs. Firbelle she was in danger?"

"You're assuming the prowler was at the party, or somehow knew about the warning," said Harriet Compton.

"Well, yes, I suppose—"

Larry turned red as his mustache and shut up. Jenny

knew why. He himself had been there, but his grandmother hadn't because her cat was sick. Elspeth had no
use for Marguerite with her air-rs an' graces. But she'd
surely never have harmed James Cox. She'd thought him
a grand man. Or so she said.

Jenny couldn't remember having mentioned to Harriet
that Elspeth wasn't at the Gileses' buffet. Apparently she
hadn't, because Harriet was still pondering Jenny's suggestion.

"Perhaps it was just that the opportunity hadn't presented itself before. The killer wouldn't have dared strike
twice within too short a period; and I shouldn't think a
woman Mrs. Firbelle's age would be out that late at night
very often, especially in a place like Meldrum. It's all
guesswork, of course."

"Yes, and the more we guess about it, the more impossible it sounds." Larry must have decided that idea was
a waste of time, because he quickly changed the subject.

"Getting back to Cox, I'm more inclined to buy your
suggestion that he simply happened to be in the wrong
place at the wrong time. As to why the prowler came back
that night of Sue's party, assuming it was the same guy,
he could have been expecting to find the carriage house
vacant, thinking Jenny was still over at the Gileses'. For
all we know, he could have been in and out of the carriage
house any number of times before Jenny moved in and
maybe hidden something there that he was anxious to get
back. Was that why you two cleared all that stuff out you
gave to the rummage sale? If somebody was after something, you were trying to make him understand you'd
searched the place and it wasn't there any more?"

"I never even thought of that," Jenny admitted. "I was tired of banging my shins every time I turned around, that's all. It never once occurred to me that one of those ghastly jardinieres might have a false bottom or whatever. But what would they hide?"

"Who knows? Jewelry, cash, drugs, stuff taken from housebreaks in the area, maybe. It was just a thought, and probably not a very good one. What do you say, ladies? Shall we get this show back on the road before everybody in Meldrum starts wondering whether we're stuck in a padded cell back there at the hospital?"

Harriet Compton started drawing on her gloves. "I'm about ready for one, myself. You're right, Larry, we'd better put this show on the road. Jenny and I are dining at the Firbelles.' It's supposed to be informal, but I daresay the matriarch expects us to arrive dressed to the eyeballs in honor of the occasion."

"No doubt," Larry drawled. "Maybe Jenny should have hung onto her hair."

18 🌿

"I'm itching to see what the front part of the Firbelles' house is like," Harriet Compton remarked as they strolled up the sidewalk in their new frocks from Louise's Boutique. They'd decided to make a formal entrance this time instead of cutting across the back yard.

"I'm not," Jenny grumbled. "I don't know why, but every time I so much as think about this place, my temperature drops about two degrees."

"And you don't mind saying so. You may not know it, young woman, but you've come a long way in the past couple of days."

"Because I'm learning to accept myself, you mean? A person more or less has to, sooner or later. I have to live with my so-called Cirak streak, so I may as well make the best of it."

"What's it telling you now, Jenny?"

"That I'd a darn sight rather be going to Elspeth Gillespie's for another high tea. What do you bet they serve us New England boiled dinner?"

Her stepmother chuckled. "You're James's daughter, all right. He was always going on about Yankees being culinary assassins. He loved to bumble around the kitchen, putting garlic into everything I cooked. I only wish I could have been a fly on the wall when he threw those fancy dinners Beth was telling us about. I can see him now, pouring champagne with his tongue in his cheek."

"Was he like that?"

"Oh, yes. James was a great clown. He'd keep a joke running for months on end if he took the notion. Sooner or later he'd have come back to the apartment and regaled me for days with his adventures in Meldrum, following me around with a half-eaten salami sandwich in his hand, roaring his head off at his own jokes and expecting me to laugh with him. And I would have, Jenny. Lord! The fools women make of themselves over men."

She put her face and the seams of her gloves straight. "Well, kid, here we are. Mind your manners and don't spit the olive pits under the table, as your father used to say."

Jenny had barely time to give her windblown hair a nervous pat before the door was opened by a maid in a black taffeta uniform and hemstitched white apron. She took their wraps.

"Will you walk into the parlor, ladies?"

Said the spider to the flies. Jenny didn't dare look at her stepmother for fear they'd both giggle.

The Firbelles' front parlor was straight out of Guided Tours of Gracious Homes. It was all there; the polished Heppelwhite furniture; the family portraits from Itinerant Signpainter to Institute of American Artists; the Lowestoft bowls heaped with burnished chrysanthemums; the firelight striking discreet gleams from the polished brass andirons.

Marguerite Firbelle was sitting in the wing chair to the right of the fireplace, exquisite in amethyst velvet, doing crewel work. Jack Firbelle lounged in the left-hand wing chair, correct in a dark Brooks Brothers suit, doing nothing. Beth Firbelle crouched on a hassock between them, dowdy in the hand-crocheted sack she'd worn to the Gileses' party, knitting on yet another disaster in the making, her yarn dangling out of the tacky drawstring bag. All three rose to greet their visitors.

"Oh, it's so good to see you!"

Beth was welcoming them as though it had been years instead of hours since they'd last been together. Was this because she felt the disagreeable scene in the church hall had somehow been her fault, and she was trying to make it up to them for that miserable drive to the hospital with Bill Giles? There was no earthly reason why she should. They'd volunteered for the job. Perhaps it was because she wanted to think of them as more her acquaintances than her aunt's. In this house, where everything spoke of Marguerite and all she stood for, that might be desperately important to a poor relation. The contrast between Beth's shabbiness and the time-mellowed beauty of her surroundings was devastating. Jenny did her best to return Beth's effusiveness.

"What's that you're knitting? It looks fascinating."

"Just a pullover. I don't know why, but I never seem to have anything to wear." Beth held out the half-finished front for Jenny to see. As expected, it looked like a lost cause already. "Sampson's were having a sale of yarn, but all the best colors were gone by the time I found out about it." Naturally.

After a genteel insufficiency of domestic sherry served by the maid in priceless Sandwich glass goblets, they went in to dinner. The food was New Englandish enough, but mercifully not boiled dinner. The maid presented first a tomato-flavored clam chowder, which tasted suspiciously like a leftover from the church luncheon. She then placed in front of Jack Firbelle a small roast of beef from which he expertly shaved paper-thin slices. Jenny could have done with less expertise and a thicker slice, but she was interested to learn that Jack had at least one talent.

Dessert was slivers of pumpkin pie served on magnificent old Tobacco Leaf plates. Coffee arrived on a silver tray back by the fire, in tiny, translucent cups some Firbelle ancestor had brought back from Canton in the clipper ship *Red Jacket*. Marguerite told her visitors about him in that light, sweet voice that tinkled like her coin silver coffee spoons.

"And now," she said, "Jack has arranged a little treat for you. He wants to show you what Beth and I think are some rather exceptional slides he's taken of our local bird life."

"We'd love to see them." Jenny didn't mean it. She was getting more edgy by the minute, watching Beth yank at that repulsive-looking yarn while Marguerite Firbelle did her lady of the manor act. Despite all the surface grace and charm, there was a tension here she found one degree short of unbearable. What was going on in this museum of a house?

"The slides sound wonderful," said Harriet Compton in her no-nonsense way, "but first I'd like to use your bathroom."

"Certainly. I'll show you." Beth jumped up from the hassock as if she, too, felt it would be a relief to escape from the parlor. "Jenny, would you like to come and see the upstairs while Jack's setting up the projector?"

She and Jenny made small talk about the dull gold wallpaper that had come from the orient as linings for tea chests while Harriet used what Beth delicately referred to as the facilities.

"Jenny, do you want to go in?" her stepmother asked when she came out.

"I'd just like to fix my hair a little." Jenny had been wearing that wig so much lately she felt slightly undressed without it.

"Use my room if you'd like," Beth urged. "Right here. That light in the bathroom isn't very good."

"Thanks, I will. Please don't wait for me. I can find my way down."

"Maybe we'd better," Beth said anxiously to Harriet Compton. "Jack can be a bit touchy sometimes."

They went downstairs, and Jenny snatched her moment of solitude. Beth's room didn't look particularly poor-relationish. It wasn't fancy or frilly—that would have been out of keeping with the quiet elegance of the house—but the spindle bed with its Martha Washington spread, the cherrywood dresser and night stand were good enough to have sent Aunt Martha into a frenzy of jealous longing.

The only incongruous note was a dolls' house, clumsily furnished with bits and pieces Beth must surely, in her inept way, have fashioned herself. It was much like one Jenny had built out of grocery cartons when she was a kid longing for a home of her own. The Plummers hadn't objected to the dollhouse because it kept young Jenny quiet and out from under foot, but she herself had realized when she was about fourteen that she couldn't live in a fantasy world forever and had passed on her dollhouse to a neighbor's child she'd begun to babysit. When she'd seen her handiwork set out with the trash a few weeks later, she hadn't felt more than a passing pang. Beth, it appeared, was less willing to give up her childish dreams.

Well, that was Beth's affair. It was high time Jenny got back to the party.

The floors of the old house were uneven, and the bedroom door had swung shut. Disoriented by her inspection of the dollhouse, Jenny made the wrong guess and found herself opening Beth's clothes closet instead of the door to the hall.

Here was another surprise. For somebody who had nothing to wear, Beth certainly took up a lot of closet space. The hangers were crammed. Perhaps much of it was Marguerite's overflow, however, for most of the frocks looked almost shockingly elegant in contrast to the homemade horrors squeezed in among them. Several were brand-new with price tags still on, and Jenny had been under Aunt Martha's influence so long she couldn't help reading the tags.

Something was wrong here. The first tag said size fourteen. How could that be? Marguerite Firbelle was as petite as Jenny herself, and Jenny took a six or an eight. The shop must have sent the wrong size, and Mrs. Firbelle hadn't yet got around to changing it. But the next was a fourteen, too, and the next, and so on down the line.

A closetful of mistakes? Ridiculous. Beth herself was a fourteen. She'd said so down at Louise's Boutique. Intrigued, Jenny shuffled through the closet. There wasn't a thing on the rack that wouldn't fit Beth, and still she drooped around saying she had nothing to wear. More mysteries!

But it was hardly polite to be snooping around your hostess's closet, and Jenny had already been away from the party too long. She found the right door and went downstairs.

"We're in the study, Jenny." Beth was at the foot of the stairs, waiting to show her the way. The room was in darkness except for a pool of light from a gooseneck lamp, which illuminated an expensive slide projector and a very annoyed operator.

"Blasted bulb's burned out, and I don't have a spare." Jack was fuming. "I'll have to call MacRae."

"Must you?" his mother protested.

"Yes, I must," he snapped back. "Where else would I get one at this time of night?"

Jack picked up the phone and dialed. "MacRae? I'm stuck with a roomful of culture vultures and no bulb for my projector. How about dropping over with one of yours? I'd be interested to see what you think of the work I'm doing with my new telephoto lens."

Jenny caught the half-patronizing, half-pleading tone of the amateur trying to put himself on level terms with the professional. Jack might sneer behind MacRae's back about commercialism, but she'd bet he was praying for a pat on the back about his new telephoto lens.

Since he could so easily have run over and gotten the bulb himself, though, she sensed that Jack's real reason for inviting MacRae was to upset his mother. Jenny also had a hunch Mrs. Firbelle knew and resented what her son was up to, but didn't dare show her feelings. The atmosphere was as tense as a telephone wire. What was going on in this stately old house, anyway?

Right now, Jack was filling in the wait with a lecture on local fauna. Harriet was listening with a polite show of interest, but Jenny wasn't paying attention at all. She was watching Beth drop stitches in the dim light. Why did the woman bother with this endless handwork when she did it so badly and when she didn't have to?

Unless the dresses crammed into that upstairs closet weren't hers after all? Could they be kept hanging there like forbidden fruit, to torture Beth with the sight of something rich women could enjoy and poor relations couldn't? Was Marguerite Firbelle really that cruel?

Or was it Jack who called the tune here? An only boy who'd been spoiled rotten all his life, as Jack obviously had, might well resent having to share his darling mama with an indigent cousin. Perhaps Marguerite bought Beth clothes out of a sense of guilt, afraid of what the neighbors would say if she didn't, and Jack kicked up a row when he saw Beth wearing them.

That would make more sense. Jack did have a nasty streak in him, anybody could see that, even though he had shown unexpected kindness to his cousin that afternoon at the luncheon. In public, with everybody watching. What happened when there was nobody around to see?

Even Mrs. Firbelle must have been relieved when the doorbell rang and the maid ushered in Lawrence MacRae. Jack stopped lecturing and started fussing. MacRae had to have his coat taken away and hung up, be given a drink he obviously didn't want. He had to admire Jack's new light meter, pronounce on the merit of some other gadget Jack was thinking of buying, and finally discuss the proper method of replacing the burnt-out bulb because the projector was such a highly developed precision instrument.

MacRae changed the bulb himself with two flicks of his capable fingers. "Okay, Jack, let's see what you've got." He was visibly sorry he'd come and eager to get the show over with. Jenny began to feel that she and Lawrence MacRae had a good deal in common.

Whatever else he might be, Jack was an excellent photographer of Bohemian waxwings. His new telephoto lens had picked out the white wing patches and rusty under-coverts, which, he explained in detail, distinguished these birds from their smaller and commoner cousins, the cedar waxwings. He showed a whole flock of cedar waxwings, too, to make sure his audience got the message.

Waxwings had charm, no doubt about that. Jenny forgot for a while she was bored and got lost in the treetops as the feathered songsters clicked by: flying, perching, nesting, eating, sleeping, delousing themselves, little reckoning that an avian Peeping Tom was recording their every winsome pose. It was, as everybody remarked at appropriate intervals, truly amazing.

Like too many amateurs, Jack didn't know enough to quit while he was ahead. After having pleased the group with his waxwings, he bored them to desperation with a miscellany of family pictures: his mother picking flowers, posing in front of Grandfather Firbelle's portrait, wandering through the garden, mother and himself beside the birdbath, taken by Beth hence a trifle out of focus.

"Who's that in the background?" Jenny asked because she hadn't said anything for some time and thought she ought to.

"Oh, that must be James Cox." Marguerite Firbelle perked up. "Jack, do show them the slides you took at the dinner party. They'll be interested because it's Jenny's house now."

Unhappily, Jack was only too willing at this point to be the obliging son. Yet another tray was fed into the projector. Taken in candlelight, the pictures were romantically dim. It was easy to see why Mrs. Firbelle wanted them shown. She herself came out exquisitely fragile in her silver brocade, her hair a shining moonlit nimbus. Beth was virtually invisible, her brown hair and mud-colored outfit blending with the shadows. James Cox was a bulk of shoulder and a flash of white shirt front, nothing of the eagle showing here.

Jack had far too many slides of the dinner party, each with Mother Firbelle much in evidence and the others

mere sepia blobs. At last he flipped to one that showed a
square of light with a man silhouetted within the frame.

"Here's Cox in the doorway waving us good night."

"That's exactly how we saw him last." Marguerite
sighed. "He often used to stand just there and look over
at this house. He said it gave him pleasure to see"—she
smiled a sad, secret smile—"where his friends lived."

Harriet Compton straightened her back, smoothed her
skirt, and threw her bomb.

"Yes, James could be quite the gay gallant when he
took the notion. I understand he cut quite a swath among
the ladies of Meldrum. Isn't that right, Lawrence?"

MacRae sounded stunned, but he gamely played her
line back. "Er—oh, yes. Yes, he did. Definitely."

The Firbelles gasped in unison. Jack was the first to get
his breath back.

"Are you saying you knew Cox?"

"How could I avoid knowing Jenny's father?" said
Harriet blandly.

"Jenny's father?"

"Hadn't you noticed the resemblance? Lawrence
spotted it right away."

"Sticks out a mile," mumbled the photographer.

"Then what's she doing here?" Jack Firbelle hurled the
question like an accusation.

"Living in the house her father left her, of course,"
Harriet Compton replied calmly.

After that, the party was definitely over. Harriet was
the only one who managed anything like a graceful farewell. Even Marguerite Firbelle's poise was shattered. Jack
glared at Jenny as if she'd been a worm in his apple,

making her so nervous she had a hard time stammering out so much as a thank you.

As for Beth, she simply faded into the background and went on with her knitting. The last words the departing guests heard as the door closed behind them were, "Oh dear. I've dropped another stitch."

19

MacRae walked Jenny and her stepmother back to the carriage house. None of them said much until they got there. Then Jenny broke the silence.

"You know what? I'm starved."

"Come to think of it, so am I," Harriet agreed. "How about it, Larry? Care to join the ladies in a sandwich?"

"Might get a bit crowded, the three of us squeezed in between the same two slices of bread."

That wasn't much of a joke, but it was enough to set them laughing. They began raiding Jenny's refrigerator, fishing out cold cuts, cheese, lettuce and tomatoes, wondering where the mustard had managed to hide itself, pouring out glasses of milk for Jenny and Larry, boiling water for Harriet's tea.

Then they were crammed in around the midget table,

eating, talking, Harriet explaining that she had decided she wanted to be there when the Firbelles realized who Jenny was. Though exactly what they should make of the family's reaction, none of them was sure. Obviously Jenny's identity was more alarming a fact than Harriet had thought it would be. They ended up making silly jokes, trying to wipe that uncomfortable scene at the Firbelles' out of their minds. They succeeded so well that they didn't realize how late it had gotten, until they heard a violent banging at the back door.

They all started. And Jenny grew cold with apprehension.

"Heavens, who could that be at this hour?" Harriet exclaimed.

Jenny giggled nervously, then tried to make a joke. "Probably your grandmother's cat, Larry, coming to take you home. I'll go."

"No, wait." Larry jumped up to forestall her. "It might be anybody."

But Jenny went, and it was only Beth Firbelle, still in that impossible crocheted potato sack, still with her drawstring bag in her hand. Beth's legs and feet were bare, her skirt rucked up over her knees. Her hair was a mess, her face flushed purple. She was panting as if she'd been running.

"Beth," Jenny cried. "What's the matter?"

"I got out."

Beth shouted the words fiercely, triumphantly, her pale eyes glittering in the light from the kitchen. "They thought they'd locked me in. Idiots! I get out whenever I want to. I'm smarter than they are. I knew all the time he wasn't James Cox. It's right here, in one of those photography books Jack's always buying. See? And I knew you looked like him. I came back and saw you after Sue Giles's party. I even brought the book."

She held up a large, slick, expensive-looking volume. Jenny could only catch a glimpse of the title, something about cinematography, before Beth flipped to the page she wanted. Yes, there was the eagle; younger than in Lawrence MacRae's photograph, black-haired, beardless, unmistakably Jason Cirak at the height of his fame.

"If you knew, why didn't you tell?" Larry demanded.

"Why should I?"

Beth's voice was too loud, too shrill. "It's my book. Don't you think I know why Aunt Marguerite brought me to Meldrum after Mummy died and they wanted to put me in the hospital like Bill Giles? I may be crazy, but I'm not too dumb to know why she's after me all the time to sign checks. Who do you think pays the bills in that house? It's mine. All mine. Aunt Marguerite's mine, bought and paid for. James Cox was trying to take her away from me."

She slammed the book shut. "Jack's mine, too. I heard them talking. They say he's going to marry you for your money, Jenny, so they can afford to put me in the nuthouse. But I'll fix that. I'll kill you the way I killed your father!"

Beth raised her arm. The drawstring bag swung down in a murderous arc.

"Jenny, look out!"

Larry snatched her out of the way, just as the bag thudded against the doorsill. They stood horrified, watching a great chip fly off the thick oaken plank. Then Larry leaped. Before Beth could swing her deadly weapon again, he had her wrestled to the ground. But her strength was incredible.

"I can't hold her," he panted. "Get help, quick. Jenny, run and bring Jack."

Having seen Bill Giles in action, Jenny didn't stop to argue. Seconds later she was across the back yard and pounding at the Firbelles' door, screaming at their open windows.

Jack rushed down, pulling a bathrobe over his pajamas. "Jenny, what's the matter?"

"It's Beth. She tried to kill me. Hurry!"

"Mother," he shouted. "Bring the capsules. Where is she, Jenny?"

"In my back yard. Larry's trying to hold her, but she's fighting like a—"

Jack wasn't waiting to hear. He was already nearly at the carriage house. Jenny heard him shout, "Turn her back to me if you can, MacRae."

By the time Jenny got to them, Jack had Beth in an expert Judo grip. Clearly, this wasn't the first time he'd had to cope with one of his cousin's insane rages. Even so, she was fighting her way out of control again when Harriet Compton rushed out to them with a roll of clothesline and the bloodstained suede jacket she'd brought from Baltimore.

"Here, wrap this around her, back to front. Pinion her arms."

All four of them together managed somehow to get the thick, soft leather around her writing, jerking body. While the men held her, Harriet and Jenny passed the rope back and forth. When Marguerite Firbelle at last made her appearance, carrying a small vial, they had Beth trussed up like a Thanksgiving turkey.

Jack took the bottle from his mother and shook out a capsule. "Come on, Beth," he coaxed. "Take your pill. It's yours. You bought it."

He and his mother pried Beth's jaws apart and forced the capsule down her throat as if they were medicating Elspeth Gillespie's cat.

"Good girl. Okay." Jack let Beth fall to the ground. "She'll quiet down in a minute. These things work fast, thank goodness. I've never seen her this bad before."

"Not even the night she murdered my father?" cried Jenny.

"She did no such thing," Marguerite Firbelle snapped back.

"Stupid." The pill was beginning to take effect. Beth lay quiet on the grass, smiling up at them drowsily, enjoying her private joke. "Of course, I killed him. I just put a brick in my bag the same way I did tonight and went back pretending I'd forgotten my scarf. When he came to the door, I let him have it. Whammo."

"Beth, you couldn't have," screamed her aunt.

"Why not? It's my brick."

Her eyes closed. Jack collapsed on the doorstep, where the broken sill showed its fresh, bright scar, and buried his face in his arms. Harriet Compton went and got the sherry bottle and a glass.

"Jack, you'd better have a drink of this. It's all we have in the house. How about you, Larry?"

"No thanks. I'm all right. I guess." Larry was still

breathing heavily, but he managed to smile as he tucked his torn shirt back under his belt. "Looks as if I'd better go get the station wagon."

Marguerite Firbelle was ready to take command again. "That will hardly be necessary. You and Jack can carry Beth that short way back to the house between you, I'm sure."

"Mrs. Firbelle," he answered, "there's no way I'm going to let you take Beth anywhere but to the hospital. Being an accessory to murder just isn't my bag. I'll drive her there myself if you want, to spare you from having to call the police ambulance, but that's as neighborly as I get."

Mrs. Firbelle tried once more. "Surely you didn't believe what she said? Beth's always making up stories. She isn't responsible."

"She's responsible for trying to brain Jenny with that brick she's got in her bag right now, because I saw her do it. Don't try to tell me you never knew how James Cox died."

"Mother only knows what she wants to know," Jack Firbelle said wearily. "Go get your car, MacRae."

20

"Twice in one day is a bit much." Jenny sighed.

She and Lawrence MacRae were alone in the station wagon, on their way back to Meldrum. Harriet Compton, Jenny hoped, was asleep in the carriage house by now. Jack Firbelle had stayed in Providence for an emergency consultation with the family lawyer, after the authorities who'd gotten hold of Beth's medical records had given him an extremely rough going-over.

What Marguerite was doing, Jenny couldn't have cared less. It had been his mother's idea, Jack claimed, to bring Beth to Meldrum after the parents who'd shielded her all her life had both died like James Cox, in so-called accidents that were never explained.

The reason, of course, was money. Beth had been left rich. Marguerite's fortune was long gone, though none of the hopeful heirs except Jack himself—not even his sister Pamela—knew that. Trying to get a power of attorney would have been too risky, so they'd simply installed Beth in Pam's old bedroom and started milking her for all she was worth. Jack had talked freely enough about the experience on their way to the hospital.

"Ever since Beth came, it's been one long nightmare. We never knew from one minute to the next if she'd be a sensible grown-up, a whining little kid, or a screaming maniac. We had to lie and scheme and cover up for her all the time. It was like living on the edge of a volcano. We knew she'd killed her mother and father. At least I did. Mother would never admit it. Sometimes I think Mother's a little crazy, too. Nothing concerns her except getting her own way. You hit the nail on the head, Jenny, when you told her that night at Sue's that there was danger around her. Mother wouldn't have stood a chance if Beth had happened to turn on her in one of those sudden wild fits. She'd keep insisting, 'Oh, Beth would never hurt me,' even when I was trying to wrestle sedatives down Beth's throat to keep her from going berserk the way she did tonight. I reminded Mother that Beth's own people used to say the same thing, right up till they died; but it was no use. You can't talk to Mother."

"What sets Beth off usually?" Larry had asked.

"Mostly it's when somebody's trying to take something of hers, or she thinks they are. She won't even wear the clothes Mother buys her because she's afraid we'll take them away to be washed or dry cleaned and she'll never get them back. She makes those ghastly duds and wears them till they fall apart, then we have to burn the rags and there's another big scene. Nobody knows what I've been through, between the two of them."

None of it would have happened if Jack hadn't been such a jellyfish in the first place, Jenny thought, but she didn't say so. It would have been too cruel, and what was the use anyway?

She spoke her mind to Larry on the long drive home, naturally. They'd talked about other things, too: themselves, their thoughts and feelings, the things they'd done, the things they'd like to do. At last Jenny had confessed what she'd been longing to tell someone, that Harriet Compton wasn't really her aunt but her stepmother.

"I suppose you two will be taking off for Baltimore after this," he'd replied, not sounding happy about the prospect.

"What for?" said Jenny. "There won't be any more midnight prowlers to scare me off, will there? After all, it was Beth I saw the night you thought I was being so mean to poor, dear Mrs. Firbelle."

"You sure know how to rub it in, don't you?"

"Well, you asked for it. Frankly, Larry, I don't know what we're going to do. I expect Aunt Harriet will go back to Baltimore fairly soon, and I'll go to visit her, of course. We want to see a lot of each other, but it's too late to start any live-together mother-and-daughter routine. She's made her own life. And even though I haven't made much of a life for myself yet, I'm working on it."

"You're going to be a famous writer."

Jenny shook her head. "After what happened to my father, I don't think I want to be a famous anything. The writing idea was just an excuse to explain living alone in the carriage house; and if you want the truth, I haven't written a line since I got there. I think what I'd like to do is keep the house and fix it up the way it ought to be. I need a place to call my own, and it's the only link I have with my father."

Jenny yawned. MacRae began singing to keep them awake, an old Scots ballad the late Colin Gillespie might have taught him.

"I hae laid a herrin' in salt.

"Lass, if ye love me, tell me noo.

"I hae brewed a fourpit o' malt,

"An' I canna come ilka day to woo. By the way, how do you like my granny?"

The sudden change of subject made Jenny laugh. "I think she's a gr-rand woman."

"Aye." The red mustache perked upward at the ends. "An' she thinks Harriet Compton's a fine, upstandin' leddy wi' nae silly air-rs an' graces aboot her. No' but what the lassie's a bonny wee thing an' a cr-redit tae the family, tinker blood or no. She thinks we ought to get better acquaintit."

"Then tell her we're planning to invite you both to a proper high tea as soon as we learn how to bake scones and crumpets."

"Och, lass, we canna wait sae long," said Lawrence MacRae. "We'll come tomorrow an' bring our ain."